"Sign The Agreement And We Can Be Married Before The Week's Out."

Aimee pushed him away. "No. I'm not signing any prenuptial agreement." She shoved the document toward him and tugged off the diamond he'd placed on her left hand earlier that evening.

"What are you doing?"

"Giving you back your engagement ring. I'm not going to marry you."

"What do you mean, you're not going to marry me? You've already said yes!"

She tipped her chin defiantly. "Well, I've changed my mind. But," she said as calmly as she could, "I think I'll take you up on your original offer."

"My original offer?"

"Yes. I'll have an affair with you instead."

Dear Reader,

Go no further! I want you to read all about what's in store for you this month at Silhouette Desire. First, there's the moment you've all been waiting for, the triumphant return of Joan Hohl's BIG BAD WOLFE series! MAN OF THE MONTH Cameron Wolfe "stars" in the absolutely wonderful *Wolfe Wedding*. This book, Joan's twenty-fifth Silhouette title, is a keeper. So if you plan on giving it to someone to read I suggest you get one for yourself *and* one for a friend—it's that good!

In addition, it's always exciting for me to present a unique new miniseries, and SONS AND LOVERS is just such a series. Lucas, Ridge and Reese are all brothers with a secret past... and a romantic future. The series begins with *Lucas: The Loner* by Cindy Gerard, and continues in February with *Reese: The Untamed* by Susan Connell and in March with *Ridge: The Avenger* by Leanne Banks. Don't miss them!

If you like humor, don't miss *Peachy's Proposal*, the next book in Carole Buck's charming, fun-filled WEDDING BELLES series, or *My House or Yours?* the latest from Lass Small.

If ranches are a place you'd like to visit, you must check out Barbara McMahon's *Cowboy's Bride*. And this month is completed with a dramatic, sensuous love story from Metsy Hingle. The story is called *Surrender*, and I think you'll surrender to the talents of this wonderful new writer.

Sincerely,

Lucia Macro
Senior Editor

Please address questions and book requests to:
Silhouette Reader Service
U.S.: 3010 Walden Ave., P.O. Box 1325, Buffalo, NY 14269
Canadian: P.O. Box 609, Fort Erie, Ont. L2A 5X3

METSY
HINGLE
SURRENDER

SILHOUETTE *Desire*®
Published by Silhouette Books
America's Publisher of Contemporary Romance

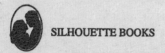

SILHOUETTE BOOKS

ISBN 0-373-05978-7

SURRENDER

Books by Metsy Hingle

Silhouette Desire

Seduced #900
Surrender #978

METSY HINGLE

is a native of New Orleans who loves the city in which she grew up. She credits the charm, antiquity and decadence of her birthplace, along with the passionate nature of her own French heritage, with instilling in her the desire to write. Married and the mother of four children, she believes in romance and happy endings. Becoming a Silhouette author is a long-cherished dream come true for Metsy and one happy ending that she continues to celebrate with each new story she writes.

To Lucia Macro
The Best Of The Best, Editor And Friend
Thanks For Taking That First Chance.

Prologue

"You expect me to sign *this?*" Aimee gripped the pre-nuptial agreement in her hand, praying the indignation in her voice masked the pain in her heart.

"I do, if we're going to be married." Peter moved toward her, and she took a step back. His lips thinned in a disapproving scowl. "At least look at the damn thing, Aimee. You'll see that I'm being more than generous."

The vise that seemed to be squeezing her heart tightened. Aimee swallowed hard, determined not to cry. "I'm sure you are." In the three months since they'd become lovers, he had been extremely generous to her, with everything—except with his love.

And it was his love that she wanted most of all.

His expression softened somewhat, and this time when he moved to put his arm around her, Aimee didn't resist. "Be reasonable, sweetheart. Just sign the thing, and then we can—"

"I'm not signing it, Peter."

His body grew rigid beside her. "Do you want to have an attorney look it over first? Is that it?"

Chilled by the distrust in his voice, Aimee moved out of his arms. She cut a glance to his face. His blue eyes had darkened to the color of steel—cold steel. "No. I don't need to have anyone look it over, because I have no intention of ever signing it."

"Why the hell not?"

"Because I don't believe in prenuptial agreements. Signing one would be tantamount to saying I don't believe the marriage is going to last."

"It probably won't. You know as well as I do that fifty percent of all marriages end in divorce."

"And fifty percent of them don't," Aimee shot back. She paused. "Why did you even bother asking me to marry you if you feel this way?"

"Because I want you."

Because he wanted her. Aimee closed her eyes and repeated the words silently. Not because he loved her.

Peter reached out and caught her by the shoulders. "Look at me, Aimee."

Opening her eyes, she lifted her gaze to his. Her pulse skittered like a colt at the raw desire she saw in his eyes.

"I want you in my bed. Tonight. Tomorrow night. Every night." Pulling her to him, he crushed the prenuptial agreement she was holding between them and captured her mouth with his.

Instinctively Aimee parted her lips, welcoming him, giving in to the dizzying sensation that only Peter could make her feel.

When he finally lifted his head, Aimee blinked. Slowly, her senses cleared, and she was able to focus on Peter's face. Her stomach clenched at the triumphant gleam in his eyes.

"You want me just as much as I want you. You said you wouldn't live with me unless we were married, so I'm offering to marry you. Don't be stubborn, Aimee. Sign the agreement, and we can be married before the week's out."

Feeling as though she had just been doused in cold water, Aimee pushed him away. "No. I'm not signing any prenuptial agreement." She shoved the crumpled document toward him and began tugging off the emerald-cut diamond he'd placed on her finger earlier that evening.

"What do you think you're doing?" he demanded.

"Giving you back your engagement ring."

"What in the hell for?"

"Because I'm not going to marry you." Scanning the room, she spotted her purse and started toward it.

Scowling, Peter threw the prenuptial agreement and ring to the floor. The stone struck the marble floor and bounced, landing on the Oriental rug. He marched after Aimee. "What do you mean, you're not going to marry me? You've already said yes!"

She tipped up her chin defiantly. "Well, I've changed my mind. Given your lack of faith in the institution of marriage, you'd probably make a lousy husband anyway. But," she said, as calmly as she could, "I think I'll take you up on your original offer."

"My original offer?"

"Yes. I'll have an affair with you instead."

One

The blanket of darkness surrounded him. Naked and alone, Peter Gallagher shivered in the empty vault. He could feel the cold penetrating his skin, stealing the last of his warmth, sapping the last of his strength. He wasn't sure how long he'd been trapped in the gallery's vault, unable to escape. But time was running out. It wouldn't be long now, he realized. The demons had finally won. Within hours, he would be dead.

Suddenly a sliver of light pierced the blackness that engulfed him. Marshaling what little energy he had left, Peter surged toward it, breaking free of the chains and stumbling into the light.

Peter came awake instantly. Opening his eyes, relief flooded him as he took in the familiar surroundings of his bedroom. His heart thundered like a racehorse's, and he forced himself to breathe slowly.

It had been that stupid dream again. He hadn't been trapped in the gallery's vault. He was home. Safe. And

Aimee still lay asleep beside him. Drawing her body close to him, he drifted back to sleep.

When he opened his eyes again, the first fingers of dawn streamed through the bedroom window. The alarm clock beside the bed started to beep. Peter reached out and hit the off button. Stealing a glance at the clock, he frowned at the illuminated numerals that declared the time to be 6:30. The internal clock that had served to rouse him shortly before six o'clock each morning for most of his thirty-six years had failed him once again.

Either his body's instinct to awaken had dissipated with age and the recurring nightmare, or sharing his bed with Aimee for the past three months had altered his lifestyle.

Who was he kidding? It had nothing to do with age or the nightmare, and everything to do with Aimee. The woman had turned his once orderly life completely upside down from the first moment he set eyes on her, at that art-gallery opening six months ago.

He still wasn't quite sure why she had captured his interest that night. With her short crop of black hair and wide ghost-blue eyes, she was not at all his usual type. Even her slender curves, nicely distributed over her five-foot-four-inch frame, were a far cry from the tall, voluptuous women who generally drew his attention. She was attractive, but by no means beautiful—except when she smiled. When that Cupid's-bow mouth of hers spread into a grin, she lit up a room and drew everyone within her radius to her.

Including him.

Of course, discovering that she was the new owner of the building he had been trying to purchase for the past several years had seemed a stroke of luck. It was also part of the reason he had pursued her.

He wanted that building. It had belonged to him once, before his divorce. He had been forced to sell it and watch his dream gallery site be turned into apartments and a gift shop, deteriorating under the hands of its new owners. But now it was within his grasp. It had taken him nearly ten years and a lot of hard work, but he had reclaimed everything he had lost, and rebuilt Gallagher's into one of the best art galleries in New Orleans. The only thing still missing was that building.

He had promised his father he would get the place back someday. The fact that his father had been dead more than nine years and would not be here to witness Peter's victory didn't matter. Maybe it was a foolish obsession. But he had made the old man a promise, and he intended to keep it. He wanted Aimee's building, and he intended to have it—even if it meant marrying again to get it.

Only he hadn't counted on wanting Aimee herself.

The object of his thoughts shifted in bed beside him, snuggling her bottom against him. Peter fought back a groan at the contact. He could feel himself growing hard at the intimacy. As always, the merest touch, the smell, even just the thought of Aimee, sent his hormones into overdrive.

When she turned down his offer of marriage, he had been sure he had somehow managed to dodge a bullet—especially when she had proclaimed they should have an affair instead. He had been confident at the time that an affair with her would not only get her to sell him the building, but would assuage his insatiable desire for her, as well.

He'd been dead wrong on both counts. Aimee wouldn't even consider selling the place. And his need, his hunger, for her had intensified, not lessened. Even now, after a night of lovemaking, he wanted her again.

Unable to resist, Peter kissed the pale skin of her shoulder, bare except for the ribbon-thin strap of her nightgown. She made that sweet little noise, something between a moan and a purr, that drove him crazy. Shifting his body closer, he tasted the skin at the nape of her neck.

"Hmmm..." Aimee murmured softly. Slowly she turned into his arms, giving him access to more silken skin. Although her eyes remained closed, a smile started at the corners of her mouth and spread. "Good morning," she whispered.

Forcing himself to move slowly, Peter slipped the strap of her nightgown down her other arm and bared her breasts. The pink, rosy nipples pebbled under his gaze, making the ache to possess her even more painful. He circled one tip with his tongue.

"Peter..." Aimee gasped.

"Morning," he said, before moving to the other breast.

Her body arched toward him, and Peter greedily accepted the invitation. His teeth grazed her nipple, eliciting another cry of pleasure from Aimee and firing his own need to bury himself inside her.

She curled her fingers in his hair, pulling his head up toward her face. "Kiss me," she commanded.

Peter obeyed, taking possession of her mouth.

Aimee parted her lips, and he drank from her sweet warmth, shutting out all traces of coldness that lingered from his dream, making him forget about the building and his need to possess it.

Making him forget everything but his need for her.

He cupped her face, shaped her breasts with his fingers. He stripped the nightgown from her body, wanting, needing to feel more of her warmth. "Ah, Aimee," he whispered. "I can't get enough of you."

"I know," she responded, her voice husky with desire. She tugged at the waistband of his pajamas, and Peter reveled, yet again, in the knowledge that her desire was always equal to his own. Only with Aimee had it ever been like this. There was so much heat between them... so much passion.

Tossing his bottoms next to her nightgown, which lay puddled on the floor, Peter moved between her legs. As he reached for the scrap of silk that guarded the treasure of her warmth, the telephone rang.

Aimee started.

Peter cursed silently. "Let it ring," he muttered as he slipped his fingers beneath her panties.

She pushed his hands away. "Peter, you have to answer it."

"No, I don't." He reached for her again.

Aimee scooted across the bed and out of his reach as the phone rang once more. "Maybe it's someone calling about the gallery."

"It isn't."

"How can you be sure?"

Peter gritted his teeth. "Because no one I know would call me at home about the gallery, and certainly not at this hour of the morning." As the phone continued to shatter the morning's silence, and his mood, Peter cursed himself for not resetting the answering machine before going to bed last night.

"What if there was a break-in?" Aimee countered.

"Then the alarm would have signaled me here—not the telephone."

"Then it's probably Liza." Aimee dived across the bed toward the nightstand where the phone continued to shrill. "I gave her your number in case she needed to reach me for anything." She retrieved the cordless phone from its cradle.

Peter promptly plucked it from her fingers. He had no intention of relinquishing Aimee to anyone this morning— and especially not to that she-devil friend of hers. "Gallagher," Peter said, knowing the word came out sounding more like a bark than a friendly greeting.

"Hello," a booming male voice with a strong foreign accent responded from the other end. "Can I speak to Aimee, *s'il vous plaît?*"

Peter's body went still. "Who in the hell is this?"

There was a pause. "This is Jacques Gaston," the other man replied, as though proud of the fact. "I am a friend of Aimee's. Is she there?"

Peter swiveled his gaze toward Aimee. She had retrieved her nightgown from the floor and was already slipping it over her head. The silky green fabric whispered along her curves as she looked at him with questioning eyes.

"Well, Jacques," Peter said coolly, "I'm afraid Aimee's busy at the moment."

Aimee frowned. She cocked her head to the side, her brow wrinkling. "Jacques? That's Jacques?" she asked, as though surprised by the call. She held out her hand for the telephone. "It's okay, Peter. I'll take it."

Peter ignored her outstretched hand and moved out of reach. "And I can't help but wonder, Jacques, what kind of 'friend' would call Aimee at another man's home at this hour of the morning."

Peter saw the anger spark, lightning-quick, in Aimee's pale blue eyes before she charged over to him. "Oh, for pity's sake. Give me the phone."

When he didn't relinquish it, Aimee snatched the phone from his fingers. She turned her back to him, furious with him for his intimidation tactics. "Hello," she said, struggling to keep her voice calm.

"*Mon amie,* it is Jacques."

"So I've gathered," she said, recognizing the voice of her new tenant. "Is something wrong, Jacques?"

"No. Nothing is wrong."

Puzzled, Aimee asked, "Was there something in particular you wanted then? I assume Liza's the one who gave you this number."

"*Oui.* Your friend Liza, she gave the number to me and asked me to call you."

"She did, did she?" Aimee wasn't sure who she was angrier with—Peter for speaking so harshly to Jacques, or her friend for having the man call Peter's house and ask for her in the first place.

"I did wish to speak with you, but you were not home. I was going to call you later, but Liza said she needed to speak with you, too. But she said your gentleman friend would not give you the message if she telephoned. So I offered to call you for her."

"I'm sure she appreciated that."

"Of course," Jacques agreed.

"Uh, Jacques . . . Would you do me a favor and put Liza on the phone, please?"

"Hello," Liza said moments later. "From the sound of things on this end, I take it my call wasn't exactly welcome. Tell me, did I wake the beast?"

Aimee cut a glance to Peter as he yanked his pajamas
from the floor, where she'd tossed them. She hated it when
Liza referred to Peter as a beast. But standing at the end of
the bed in only pajama bottoms, with his arms folded across
his chest and a scowl on his handsome face, he did look like
a beast—an angry beast. "No, you didn't. We weren't
sleeping, we..." Aimee caught herself. She could feel the
flush climb her cheeks as she realized she'd almost said they
had been making love. She looked down at the rumpled
sheets on the bed and felt a moment of regret. Were it not
for Liza's call, they would be making love at this moment.

"Yes? You were what?"

Irritation rippled over Aimee at the amusement in her
friend's voice. "Never mind." Turning away from the bed
and Peter, Aimee walked across the room and looked out
the window of the plush penthouse condo. The sun was already high in the sky, gleaming hotly on the waters of the
Mississippi River. Summer in New Orleans was always a
scorcher. This one was no different. But it was nothing
compared to the heat and passion of her relationship with
Peter—a relationship that her friend feared would cause
Aimee heartbreak. Still, Liza's concern for her didn't excuse the other woman's attempts to make Peter jealous. Besides, even if Liza succeeded and Peter did display
occasional signs of possessiveness, it didn't mean he loved
her. And his love was what she wanted.

"This better be good, Liza. I gave you this number in case
there was an emergency."

"Would you classify a leaking pipe in one of the apartments as an emergency?"

"Considering the fact that there've been at least half a
dozen leaking pipes in that building since I inherited it, I
guess it would depend on just how bad the leak is." Aimee
sighed, some of her initial irritation giving way to concern.
"So tell me. Is it really bad?" she asked, dreading playing
plumber again, and hoping it was something as simple as
changing a gasket. She'd really gotten that one down pat.

And she certainly didn't want to dip into her meager funds to pay a plumber's fee.

"A small but steady stream."

Aimee bit back a groan. "All right. Whose apartment is it this time?"

"Yours."

"Mine?" Aimee swallowed. "But how would you know my pipe was leaking? Unless..."

"Unless it was leaking into the shop," Liza continued, confirming Aimee's worst fears. "It is."

"Oh, my God! Then that means the shop's—"

"A bit wet at the moment," Liza finished for her.

"How bad is it?"

"Bad enough. I shut off the water, but I'm afraid some of Simone's feathered masks are ruined. A couple of ceiling tiles fell and cracked one of the glass cases. I thought you might want to get down here and survey the damage before you call the insurance company."

"I don't have insurance anymore," Aimee advised her friend. "I canceled the policy last month." To save money, she added silently.

"I'm sorry, Aimee." There was no mistaking the genuine remorse in her friend's voice. "But it really isn't all that bad. I was just coming downstairs to get the morning paper when I heard the ceiling tile fall. And this Jacques fellow showed up, looking for you, and offered to help." Judging from her friend's tone, Aimee guessed her new tenant hadn't exactly won Liza over. "Except for a little water, most of the stuff is okay. I'll start mopping up. With any luck, we'll probably still be able to open the shop this afternoon."

"Thanks, Liza. I owe you one."

"Forget it. Just kiss the beast goodbye and get your rear over here before I end up chipping my nails."

Aimee smiled, some of her initial panic easing. "All right. I'll be there in a couple of minutes." She hit the off button and tossed the phone on the bed. "I have to go home."

"Why?" Peter asked, following her across the room. "What did Liza want? And who in the hell is Jacques?"

"Liza called because there's a pipe leaking in my apartment." Unable to locate her clothes, Aimee dropped to her knees and looked under the bed. "Jacques is a new tenant. He moved in two days ago, into Hank's old apartment."

"You never mentioned anything about a new tenant. And what's with the phony accent?"

"It's not phony. Jacques is from France." She retrieved a silver earring.

Peter walked over to the edge of the bed and stood next to her crouched figure. "Would you slow down a second and tell me what it is you're looking for?"

"My clothes." She headed for the living room. There she spied her jeans and blouse, on the Aubusson rug, next to Peter's shirt. Aimee looked up, seeing once again the two paintings—a Picasso and a child's watercolor. Her heart swelled, as it had the previous evening, at the sight of the priceless work of art mounted alongside a child's rendering of a flower. The picture had been a gift from a fatherless boy participating in the summer art program Peter had sponsored.

She had been stunned to see the painting in Peter's elegantly furnished home. "I bought it because I liked it," Peter had said when she questioned him. "I'm a businessman, not a sentimentalist. It's an investment," he had added defensively, obviously embarrassed that she considered his actions kind. "I've got a good eye for art, and I think Tommy might give Picasso a run for his money some day."

Despite his protests, the gesture had warmed her heart. It was this gentle side of Peter, that part of him that accorded a young boy's drawing the same reverence he did a Picasso, that had made falling in love with him inevitable.

Reaching for her jeans, Aimee winced as her bare foot came down on one of the buttons she'd torn from Peter's shirt in her haste the previous evening. She bit her lip, remembering how aggressive she'd been.

"I don't understand what the big rush is. You've had leaking pipes before. Get Liza to put a pan under it for now."

Lost in her thoughts, Aimee hadn't heard Peter come up behind her. She looked up at him, and her heart tripped faster at the warmth in his eyes.

"Let me fix you some breakfast first, then I'll take you home."

"I'm sorry, Peter. I don't have time. The pipe leaked through at least one ceiling tile that I know of, and it fell into the shop and cracked one of the display cases. That means I've got at least some ceiling damage, not to mention a shop full of water, and Liza said some of Simone's feathered masks were ruined." The panic came back to her in a rush, and Aimee immediately went into motion. She scooped up her jeans from the floor. "Heaven knows how much of the other merchandise has been damaged, and I don't have any idea what kind of shape my apartment's going to be in. I've got to get over there."

Peter caught her by the shoulders as she reached for her blouse. "Hey, slow down a minute."

"But I—"

Peter placed a silencing finger over her mouth. "I want you to take a deep breath."

She did as he instructed, and her nerves settled somewhat.

"All right. Now, did Liza turn off the water?"

Aimee nodded.

"Good." He tugged her into his arms and held her head to his chest. He stroked her hair. "I know this guy who's a plumber. Why don't I give him a call and have him take care of it for you? He'll have it fixed in no time."

Aimee pulled away from him. "Peter, I can't afford a plumber."

"You don't have to." He massaged the back of her neck with his fingers. "I'll take care of it for you."

"No," Aimee said firmly. She stepped out of his arms and away from his touch. "I can't let you do that."

Peter frowned. "Why not?"

"You know why. Because it's my building and my responsibility. Not yours." Ignoring his sullen expression, Aimee started for the bedroom.

Peter followed. "Then make it my responsibility. Sell me the building. I've offered to buy the place from you before. The offer's still good. Just say the word and I'll take it off your hands."

"I don't *want* it taken off my hands. It's my home," she said, kicking her nightgown aside. Conscious of Peter's gaze on her naked back, Aimee pulled her shirt over her head and then reached for her jeans.

"All right. Forget about the building, then. But don't go rushing home. Not yet." He brushed his lips against her nape and moved his body behind hers. "Stay, Aimee," he whispered.

Aimee could feel his arousal pressed against her. Her breath quickened. She curled her fingers into the jeans she was holding. Oh, how she wanted to stay, how tempting he made it for her to forget her responsibilities and be with him. "I can't," she said finally, breaking free of the sensual spell of his nearness.

Peter's mouth stilled on her neck, and Aimee was keenly aware of the loss of his warmth as he released her. "Can't or won't, Aimee?"

She knew he didn't understand her not allowing him to pay for the plumber, any more than he had understood her reasons for not marrying him. Sometimes she wasn't even sure she understood them herself. All she knew was that she loved him and it was his love she wanted in return—not his money or his help fixing her building or even in launching her art career.

But Peter didn't believe that, because he was convinced everyone wanted something, everyone had an angle. She slipped into her jeans, then turned to face him. "Can't. I've got a leaking pipe to fix."

Peter remained silent, his face a stone mask, as she located her sandals and slid them onto her feet.

He yanked open his closet door and came out with a sport shirt and slacks. Tossing the clothes on the bed, he stripped off his pajama bottoms. Except for low-rise teal briefs, he was naked. Lean and solid, muscles rippling across his chest and shoulders as he moved, he reminded her of an ancient warrior. "Give me a minute to get dressed and I'll take you home."

"Don't worry about it," she said, averting her gaze. "It's just a couple of blocks."

He ignored her and pulled on his slacks. "I said I would see you home."

"Peter, please. I don't want to argue with you. I don't have time. I have to go. Besides, you and I both know I can be home before the valet can even bring your car around." Grabbing her purse from the dresser, she rushed over to him and gave him a quick kiss. "See you later?"

"Sure," he said.

But from the look of frustration on his face, Aimee wasn't so sure that she would.

The woman was driving him crazy, Peter admitted silently. He shut the door to Gallagher's and headed out into the summer heat. Despite the smoldering temperature and choking humidity, he strode at a clipped pace along the battered sidewalks of the French Quarter. A trickle of perspiration dotted his brow, and he loosened the tie at his neck.

How had his life gotten so out of hand? What had started out as a simple plan had turned into something a great deal more complicated. Any way he looked at it, Aimee Lawrence was tying him up in knots.

He didn't like it. He liked even less the fact that he couldn't seem to stop thinking about her.

The sun gleamed down, hot and punishing, and Peter slowed his steps. He glanced about the nearly empty streets and grimaced. Even the tourists who had been foolish enough to visit the city in the middle of June had enough sense to avoid the oppressive afternoon heat. Only idiots like himself were out roaming the streets in the sweltering sun.

And he did feel like an idiot, Peter acknowledged. He should be at Gallagher's, uncrating the Matisse he had battled for so fiercely at the last auction. Instead, he was wandering through the streets of the French Quarter and thinking about Aimee.

Pausing, Peter wiped at his brow with his handkerchief and then glanced up. He frowned when he discovered he was standing in front of Aimee's building. That in itself demonstrated just how completely she had been occupying his thoughts. He hadn't planned to come here today. He had promised himself he was going to stay away from her until she came to her senses . . . until she came to him.

Only Aimee hadn't come. She hadn't bothered to call him either.

The frustration he had experienced that morning came back to him in a rush, along with the anger. He was still angry with her, he realized—not for leaving him when he'd asked her to stay, but for refusing his help.

It was one thing for Aimee to refuse to sell him the building. After all, he had been less than honest with her. She didn't know that he was the unnamed buyer who had tried to purchase the place from her when she first inherited it.

She certainly hadn't known then, and didn't know even now, that the building had once belonged to him and he had sworn it would be his once again. Besides, he was sure she would be less than pleased to learn that the reason he had sought her out in the first place was to convince her to sell him the place. And he had no doubt that, if she ever learned that part of the reason he had asked her to marry him was to regain control of the building, she would be furious.

Still, his offers to help her with the repairs had been genuine and had had nothing to do with his interest in the building. He'd made the offers because he cared about her. He didn't like seeing her work so hard to keep the place up. And he was getting damned tired of her throwing his offers to help back in his teeth.

Seeing his scowling reflection in the shop's window, Peter tried to school his expression. He didn't want to attempt to reason with Aimee while he was still angry.

But he was angry...and confused. Nothing about Aimee or his feelings for her fit in his orderly life or in his plans. And for an artist with a bohemian spirit, Aimee Lawrence was proving to be one of the most stubborn people he'd ever come up against. He didn't understand her...and he certainly didn't understand her refusing his offer of marriage and opting for an affair instead. It just didn't make any sense.

Not for one minute did he believe she'd turned him down because he'd presented her with the prenuptial agreement. Everyone used the things these days. It was the smart way to do business. If he had had any sense, he would have insisted on one in his first marriage. If he had, the building would still be his and he never would have asked Aimee to marry him in the first place.

And if he had had a prenuptial agreement the first time around, he certainly wouldn't be standing here in ninety-plus-degree heat, contemplating asking Aimee to marry him for the second time.

Because he was going to ask her again. He already knew that. In truth, he'd known it for some time. He was simply tired of waiting. He wanted to get on with his plans to expand Gallagher's, and he needed her building to do it. There simply was no other piece of property that would do. He wanted that building, and he intended to have it.

Only somewhere along the way in the past few months, he'd discovered that he wanted Aimee, too.

The problem was, he wasn't quite sure whether this need to bind her to him stemmed from his obsession with reclaiming the building or from his obsession with the woman herself.

Obsession.

He didn't particularly like the word, but it aptly described the way she made him feel, the burning hunger to be with her that seemed to have become a part of him, the way

she filled his thoughts and haunted his days when he wasn't
with her.

Yes, Aimee Lawrence had become an obsession for
him...an obsession he didn't understand...an obsession
that rivaled his driving need to reclaim the building that had
once belonged to him. That, in itself, made her dangerous.
What was even more alarming was that he had yet to get a
handle on Aimee or figure out what her angle was.

Because he was sure she had an angle. Everyone did. His
ex-wife, Leslie, certainly had. She'd used him as her spring-
board to fame in the art world, then dumped him and taken
most of his assets with her when she found someone who
could take her to the next stage of stardom.

So what was Aimee's angle? It certainly hadn't made any
sense for her to turn down the sure thing marriage to him
had offered by refusing to sign the prenuptial agreement.

And it made even less sense for her to turn down his offers to help with the building's repairs. Unless she thought
that, when she refused his financial assistance and his offer
of marriage, he would relent and agree to launch her career
as an artist.

Peter steeled himself. The face that looked back at him
from the window was cold, controlled once again. He might
have broken one of his rules by considering marriage again,
but launching Aimee as an artist and making her into a star
was something he had no intention of ever doing. Never
again would he put his livelihood at risk that way. And never
again would he allow any woman to use him. No, if Aimee
had any plans for him to be her starmaker, she was sadly
mistaken.

If Aimee made it as an artist, she was going to have to do
it without his help. In the meantime, he would marry her. As
his wife, she would accept his help in refurbishing the
building. With a little persuasion she would agree to his
opening another branch of Gallagher's here. He would
compensate her fairly for the place. And when the chemistry between them had burned itself out, as he knew it would,

he would settle with her fairly. Only this time, he intended to be the one who got the building.

Peter looked at the closed sign displayed in the shop's window and frowned. It wouldn't be the first time that Aimee had closed up the place on a whim. Whenever the urge to spend the day at the beach or play tourist struck her, she would shut down the shop and be off in a flash.

She was a lousy businesswoman, and everyone knew it...including her tenants. That was one of the reasons she was always short on cash. It was also the reason she had agreed to allow Liza to live in one of the building's apartments rent-free in exchange for running the shop.

Arcing his hands around his eyes, Peter peered through the window. Although the lights were on, there was no sign of Aimee or Liza. He could see a ladder parked in the center of the room next to a display case. Water stains splattered the wall directly behind it.

Peter grimaced. Guilt pricked at him. Evidently the damage was worse than he had suspected. And, no doubt, Aimee would be trying to make the repairs herself, probably had been most of the day.

It was just one more reason for him to insist that Aimee marry him. Surely, as his wife, she would accept his help. He started to ring the bell, so that Aimee could release the locks on the building's main door and allow him to enter, but decided to try the doorknob instead. It turned on the first try, giving him complete access to the building.

Swearing again at Aimee's continued lack of caution, Peter started up the steep stairway leading to her apartment. The woman needed a keeper, he told himself. Yet another reason to insist she marry him. At least he would make sure she was safe—even if that only meant locking the doors.

He turned the corner and started down the hall to Aimee's apartment. As usual, not only was the door to her apartment unlocked, it was open.

He stepped inside the living room, too occupied with his thoughts of Aimee to think about the memories and plans that this particular apartment held for him. He followed the haphazard trail of how-to manuals that led from the living room to the kitchen. Stooping down, he retrieved a worn red-covered volume entitled *Save A Fortune—Do Your Own Plumbing Repairs*. He shook his head, marveling at the strength of Aimee's determination.

"Oh, Jacques, you're a lifesaver."

Peter paused at the sound of Aimee's voice coming from the direction of her bedroom.

"Nonsense, *mon amie*. It was nothing."

Peter went still at the distinctly male and decidedly French voice that responded.

"But it's true. I really don't know what I would have done without you."

Anger began to simmer inside him. Anger, and some inexplicable fear of what he was about to discover. Still holding the book, Peter moved purposefully toward the bedroom. The door was open, and the bed was piled high with an assortment of towels, soaps and toiletry items.

But there was no Aimee. And no Jacques.

"Ah, *mon amie*, something tells me you would have managed just fine without me. But if you wish to think of me as your hero, then who am I to argue?"

Aimee laughed, and Jacques joined in.

Peter gritted his teeth. He liked the man's laughter even less than he liked his foreign accent, he decided. Crossing the room, he came to a stop at the doorway of Aimee's bathroom, just in time to see her raise herself up on her toes and kiss the other man on the cheek.

"Am I interrupting?" Peter asked, in a voice that was a great deal more civil than he was feeling.

Aimee jumped. "Peter! What a nice surprise. I wasn't expecting you." She rushed over and brushed her mouth against his.

"Obviously." He slipped his arm around Aimee's waist and anchored her to his side. Given the way the other man was looking at her, it would have provided him with a great deal of pleasure to wipe the smile off the Frenchman's face.

"Peter, this is Jacques Gaston. He's the new tenant I told you about." Still smiling, Aimee continued, "Jacques, this is Peter—"

"Gallagher." Peter finished the introduction for her. With a feral smile, he extended his hand. "Aimee's fiancé."

Two

—

Stunned, Aimee opened her mouth, then clamped it shut. She could feel the flush climb her cheeks at Jacques's questioning gaze.

"I had not realized Aimee was engaged," Jacques said, breaking the awkward silence. "Congratulations, Monsieur Gallagher. You are indeed a lucky man. And you, *mon amie*," he continued, "you should have told me you were affianced."

"I'm not," Aimee said. As she recovered from the initial shock of Peter's declaration, her temper started to rise. Did he think by proclaiming them to be engaged he could make her sign that stupid prenuptial agreement and marry him? If he did, he had another thought coming.

"But, I do not understand," Jacques replied, his bewilderment evident.

He wasn't the only one, Aimee fumed silently. She tried to pry herself free from Peter's side, but his fingers were like talons of steel, keeping her pinned to him.

"What Aimee means is that it's not official yet," Peter explained.

Aimee shot a fiery glance toward Peter at the out-and-out lie. "What I mean is that we are *not* engaged—" She hesitated at his pained expression. Her chest tightened as she glimpsed the sadness hidden beneath his hard facade. As always, Peter's vulnerability was her undoing. The anger drained from her as quickly as it had come. "Yet," she found herself adding.

Peter's fingers eased their death grip on her waist, but he didn't release her. "You see, Aimee hasn't actually agreed to marry me yet." He cupped her jaw with his free hand, gently turning her so that she was forced to look into his eyes. "But I have every intention of changing her mind."

He stroked her bare arm. It was an innocent gesture, but one that set off tiny currents of sensation in her body. It had always been like this with Peter—the electricity, the heat—right from the beginning. As she looked into his eyes, she could feel it happening again, the flush of warmth, the excitement. From the first time she looked into his blue eyes, all hungry and hot as he watched her, she had responded with an answering need. Tendrils of heat unfurled in her stomach, flowed between her thighs.

She had felt like Cinderella that first night, and Peter had been her prince. She had been powerless against her feelings for him, and had fallen in love with him almost from the start. His swift and relentless pursuit of her, followed by the proposal of marriage, had only added to the fairy-tale feeling.

Except Peter hadn't offered her a glass slipper or a place in his art kingdom where they would live happily ever after. She would easily have forgone both those things, if he had only offered her his love.

He hadn't. Instead, he had offered her a contract, one without promise or even hope for the future—a piece of paper that said he didn't believe in love. That he didn't love her.

It had hurt. It still hurt. Yet she continued to love him. And there were moments, like when he awakened from one of the bad dreams that plagued him, or like now, when she sensed the yearning in him... It was at these times that she was sure that Peter not only wanted her love, but needed it, too.

It was these moments that made her decide to continue her relationship with Peter...that gave her hope that he might fall in love with her one day...that made her bite her tongue now and give credence to the false impression he had just given Jacques.

"Shame on you, Aimee."

Aimee pulled her thoughts back to the present at the sound of Jacques's voice. "I beg your pardon?"

"You allowed me to boast to you about my exhibition and never told me about your own."

"Jacques, what are you talking about?" Aimee asked, genuinely confused by the direction of the conversation.

"I mean, Peter here is the owner of Gallagher's, no?"

"Yes."

"Then, surely, as your almost-fiancé, his gallery will be hosting an exhibit of your works."

Peter's fingers stilled on her arm. Pain lanced through Aimee as she felt his body stiffen beside her. Quickly she stepped away from him, feeling as though she had just taken an arrow in the heart.

"Gallagher's doesn't carry my work," Aimee said evenly.

"But I don't understand," Jacques began. "I thought that since you and Peter were...that is, if you are soon to be married..."

"It's all right, Jacques." Aimee knew exactly what Jacques had thought. The same thing everyone else had thought. That if she and Peter were sleeping together, then surely he would be displaying her work.

Only Peter had made it plain from the start that he had no interest in her as an artist—only as a woman. While that in itself was exciting, it did have its drawbacks—especially when she wanted so desperately to earn her living with her art. Still, from what little she had learned of his past, that he had been married to an artist and had been badly burned by the experience, she did understand somewhat. He had sworn never to mix business with pleasure again.

Though she was disappointed, she had agreed to his terms. It had been the only way to prove to Peter that it was *him* she loved and that her feelings had nothing to do with what he could do for her career. Still, his rejection of her as an artist had hurt. It had made her question whether it was the idea of representing an artist with whom he was involved that he found objectionable, or whether it was the work itself. While she knew she would never be another Ida Kohlmeyer, she had hoped to find a home for her work—if for no other reason than to feel worthy of the name *artist*. The fact that her art had yet to capture any significant dealer's eye only added to her sense of insecurity.

"It's not a reflection on Aimee as an artist," Peter explained, as though he had sensed her thoughts. "I simply make it a policy not to represent the work of any artist with whom I'm personally involved."

"But surely, after seeing Aimee's work, her talent—"

"Oh, my, I certainly could use something cool to drink," Aimee proclaimed, feigning thirst in an attempt to change the subject. "What about you, Jacques? The least I can do is offer you something to drink for helping me with that pipe." Slipping her arm through his, Aimee led him through the bedroom and headed toward the kitchen.

"Forgive me, Aimee," Jacques whispered as they made their way to the front of the apartment. "I did not mean to open old wounds."

Aimee looked up at the handsome Frenchman, moved by his sensitivity. She gave his arm a light squeeze. "I know."

Why, she asked herself for the dozenth time, couldn't she have given her heart to someone like Jacques? He was certainly more handsome than Peter. With dark blond hair that fell past his collar, and laughing brown eyes, he turned female heads wherever he went. He was kind, caring. And, as a fellow artist, he understood and shared her own passion for making art. To top it off, he had been interested in her.

But it wasn't Jacques who made her heart race. It wasn't Jacques who could look at her across a crowded room and make her breath catch, her body tremble with longing. It wasn't Jacques she loved.

It was Peter.

"Chin up, little one," Jacques murmured, breaking into her thoughts. "I'm the one who should be wearing the long face."

"You? Why?"

The smile in his eyes spread across his lips. "Because here I finally find the woman of my dreams, only to have her turn me down because she prefers to give her heart to a beast."

"You've been listening to Liza," she said accusingly, then ruined the reprimand by chuckling.

"Laugh if you will. But perhaps I am the lucky one, after all, to escape in one piece."

"What do you mean?"

"Judging by your Peter's expression when he came in, I think he would have liked very much to rip my heart from my chest. He's a hard man, your Peter." His grin eased the impact of what he was saying. "But then, I suspect you already know that. He needs your gentleness. Whereas I, I am a man renowned for his gentle nature. Ask anyone who knows me."

"You mean any female who knows you," Aimee told him, her mood lightening at his teasing.

"Especially any female."

Still laughing, Aimee entered the kitchen. Her gaze swept over the room, and she was glad once again that she had painted the old wooden cabinets white. The room looked brighter, more spacious, than before, and the colorful spice print that she'd painstakingly applied to the walls lifted her spirits. A smile still on her lips, she turned to Jacques. "Now what can I get you to drink?" Opening the refrigerator, she inventoried its contents. "I have ice tea, apple juice, lemonade..."

"Any wine?"

"Sure." How European, Aimee mused. She retrieved the bottle that the clerk at the wine store had insisted should be stored lengthwise on the shelf. She cut a glance to Peter, who was standing in the middle of the room, his arms crossed, his face unsmiling. "What about you, Peter? Would you like some wine?"

"No."

She handed the bottle to Jacques and directed him to the drawer that held the corkscrew. She turned her attention to Peter again. "Something else, then? The lemonade's fresh. I made it myself this morning."

"No, thanks."

He followed her across the room to the cabinet, and Aimee was all too aware of him standing behind her. Reaching over her head, he removed two wineglasses from the top shelf that were just out of her reach and handed them to her. When she would have taken them and turned away, he held on to the stems, forcing her to look up at him. "What I would like is to talk to you—alone."

Aimee looked from his mouth to his eyes. She saw the demand there . . . and the heat. Her pulse quickened in response. She leaned toward him.

"This is an excellent wine, Aimee. Are you sure you don't want to save it for a special occasion?"

Aimee jerked back, chastising herself for reacting as she did to Peter's nearness. He released the glasses, and she hurried across the room with them. "This *is* a special occasion," she said, forcing a smile into her voice that she was far from feeling. "Thanks to you, my pipe's fixed and I saved a small fortune in plumber's fees." A small fortune she didn't have, and was unlikely to have at any time in the future, Aimee added silently. She could only hope that she would be as lucky at repairing the ceiling tiles.

"Is this a private party, or can anyone join in?" Liza asked from the doorway. She sauntered into the room, her long, sleek legs exposed to full advantage by cuffed khaki shorts. With her crisp white blouse and her long blond hair pulled back in a neat French braid, Liza looked as cool and fresh as a summer breeze.

Aimee glanced down at her own denim cutoffs and her nicely shaped, but noticeably shorter, legs. She noted the smudge of grease on her faded art T-shirt. She grimaced, all too aware of the contrast between herself and her elegant friend...and wondered, not for the first time, how Peter could possibly have chosen her over Liza the night they met.

"A beautiful woman is always welcome," Jacques said. Taking Liza's hand, he brought it to his lips.

"My, my, you are a smooth one," Liza said.

"I will take that as a compliment, *mademoiselle*. It is *mademoiselle*, isn't it? I assumed you asked for my assistance this morning because there was no Monsieur O'Malley."

Liza shot him a look that Aimee had seen her friend use in the past to freeze men in their tracks. It didn't work on Jacques.

"You shut the door on me so quickly this morning, I did not have an opportunity to officially introduce myself to you. Jacques Gaston. Artist *extraordinaire*."

"Not only smooth, but modest, too," Liza quipped, withdrawing her hand.

"I see no reason for false modesty," Jacques returned. A megawatt smile spread across his handsome face. "Do you?"

Aimee bit back a laugh at the wary arch of her friend's brow. Like most men, Jacques was obviously drawn to the other woman's beauty. That was something Liza herself considered a flaw, since most people failed to see past the physical loveliness to the woman inside.

She cut a glance to Jacques, and grinned at his captivated expression. Whether Liza wanted it or not, she had herself another conquest. The truth was, Aimee had yet to meet a member of the male species who hadn't succumbed to Liza's beauty and charm.

Except Peter.

Although he had met her and Liza at the same party, Peter had never once shown any interest in her gorgeous friend. *She* had been the sole object of his attention.

As Liza and Jacques continued to spar, Aimee looked across the room at Peter. Leaning against the countertop, his arms folded over his chest, he appeared bored and even irritated by Liza's appearance—not the least bit affected by her friend's beauty. For some reason, the thought filled Aimee with pleasure, made her feel special. Surely, if Peter's interest in her was merely physical, he would have found Liza equally appealing.

As though sensing her scrutiny, Peter shifted his gaze to Aimee. His eyes darkened to a smoky blue, reminding her of storm clouds gathering before a squall. He stared at her mouth, her throat, then dropped his gaze to her breasts. Braless, her nipples hardened against her T-shirt.

Aimee swallowed as his gaze dropped lower still. Her stomach quivered in response, and she could feel the warm tenderness gathering between her thighs.

"No thanks, Mr. Gaston," Liza was saying. "I gave up being interested in seeing a man's etchings ... er, paintings, when I was still in high school," she added coolly.

The ice in her friend's voice enabled Aimee to turn away, breaking the sensuous spell Peter cast over her with one of his steamy looks.

"I promise you, mine are worth seeing," Jacques said, seemingly unperturbed by Liza's barb.

"Like I said, I'm not interested in seeing your paintings. But I'm sure Aimee would love to see them."

Aimee narrowed her eyes at the triumphant note in Liza's voice. She caught the smug smile her friend tossed Peter's way. For the life of her, Aimee didn't understand why Liza insisted Peter was using her, or why her friend remained furious with Peter for his refusal to marry without the prenuptial agreement. Whatever the reason, Aimee was certain that Liza's attempts to make Peter jealous were not the answer to her dilemma. Jealousy didn't necessarily equal love. Although she had told her friend as much on numerous occasions, it hadn't stopped the blond beauty from trying to elicit that reaction from Peter.

"After all, Aimee's an artist," Liza said sweetly. "It's something the two of you have in common."

Aimee cut a glance to Peter. From his thunderous expression, she knew Peter had risen to Liza's bait once again.

"Ah, but Aimee has already seen my paintings," Jacques said smoothly.

"Has she now?" Peter asked, his mouth tightening into an angry line.

"Yes," Jacques replied offhandedly.

Aimee nearly groaned, wishing Jacques had explained that she had seen the paintings when he moved into the building, two days before. Obviously, from the looks on both Liza's and Peter's faces, they had jumped to a far less innocent conclusion—one that Aimee refused to dignify with an explanation.

"But you, Liza, have not seen my work." Evidently not the least concerned by the scowl on Peter's face, Jacques refilled Liza's wineglass. "Sure you won't change your mind?"

"Quite sure." Liza set her glass down firmly on the countertop. The crystal clinked against the ceramic, the sound loud in the tension-filled silence. Tipping up her chin at a haughty angle, Liza turned to Aimee. "Simone asked me to let you know she's having a problem with the door to her apartment. It's sticking again, and she swears if she closes the thing she won't be able to open it. She's afraid to leave her apartment, because she's convinced she won't be able to get back inside."

Aimee sighed. As much as she loved Aunt Tessie's old building, the place really was a landlord's nightmare and a repairman's dream. If one had the money to pay for the repairs, that is. Unfortunately, she didn't. Still, she knew she could never part with the place. It meant too much to her. It represented too many dreams.

"It's probably the heat and humidity making the wood swell," Jacques informed her.

"You think so?" Aimee asked hopefully. Surely one of her father's manuals would have instructions on what to do to fix swollen wood, she thought. Already her thoughts were racing ahead to how to handle the repair.

"I think it is quite possible. It is not uncommon for an older structure like this one to have such a problem. It is a simple matter to fix. You remove the door, sand down its edges, and then, *voilà!* The door fits once again."

"Oh, Jacques, you're a genius," Aimee declared. Relief flooded through her.

"I thought you were an artist," Liza said accusingly.

Jacques smiled slowly. "I am a man of many talents, Liza. Art is just one of them."

The look he gave her friend could have melted ice, but Liza's spine only seemed to grow stiffer.

"If you do not believe me, ask Aimee."

Peter surged forward and grabbed the front of Jacques's shirt. "And just what in the hell do you mean by that?"

"Peter!" Aimee raced over to him and tugged at his arm.

Peter ignored her. He curled his fist in the other man's shirt. "Answer me, dammit."

Jacques threw his head back and laughed. "Ah, *mon amie,* I think your almost-fiancé will not settle for a long engagement. He has the fever in his blood where you are concerned. And when a man gets the fever in his blood for a woman—" his gaze swept from Aimee to Liza, then back again "—he will stop at nothing until he has claimed her as his."

Peter could feel his face flush. Shaking Aimee off his arm, he drew back his fist. "Why, you son of a—"

Aimee and Liza both screamed.

Jacques blocked the blow. "*Mon Dieu!* Get hold of yourself, Gallagher. I was talking about my talent for fixing broken pipes—not as Aimee's lover."

The pipe? Peter pulled back on the second punch, almost losing his balance in the process. He released his hold on Jacques's shirt. *The man had been talking about fixing a pipe?*

Jacques rolled his eyes heavenward. "You are hot-tempered for an American. You must have the fiery blood of the French mixed in your veins." He smoothed the rumpled lines of his shirt. "Do you not remember? I had just finished helping Aimee change the leaking pipe in her bathroom when you arrived."

Peter thrust his hands through his hair. *What in the hell is the matter with me?* He had come here intent on convincing Aimee to marry him. Instead, he'd almost decked a guy for fixing her leaking pipe and managed to earn himself another dark scowl from Aimee.

"I'm so sorry, Jacques," Aimee said. "I can't imagine what got into Peter."

Peter frowned. To make matters worse, Aimee was falling all over the man with apologies, and he still wanted to take a shot at the Frenchman's arrogant chin. Fighting the urge to wipe the smile from the other man's face, Peter jammed his fists into his pockets.

"Honestly. Peter's not usually so...so..."

"Jealous," Liza supplied.

"Quick-tempered," Aimee said.

"I am not quick-tempered, and I am not jealous!" Peter glared at Aimee. "And I'll be damned if I'm going to apologize to this egotistical Frenchman or let you apologize for me. For two cents, I'd still like to knock the guy's lights out, and I will if he doesn't stop leering at you."

"For once, Peter, I agree with you. He is an egotistical Frenchman," Liza quipped.

Peter ignored her. Enraged, he balled his hands into fists. He moved within inches of Jacques and leaned closer, making sure the Frenchman saw the anger and violence in his eyes. "In fact, if you and that little blond she-devil don't get out of here within the next two minutes and let me talk to Aimee alone, I may do just that."

Without waiting for a reply, Peter grabbed Aimee by the arm and marched her into the living room, where he pulled open the door to the apartment and waited.

"Come along, Liza." Jacques took the she-devil by the arm and propelled her toward the door. "Why don't you show me where Mademoiselle Simone's apartment is, and I'll take a look at that door for her?"

"Thank you, Jacques," Aimee said softly. "Tell Simone I'll be up to check on it later."

Aimee closed the door behind them. Peter reached over her and turned the lock. Aimee spun around, but before she could walk away, Peter planted both of his hands firmly against the door, trapping her within the circle of his arms.

Her hands came up defensively; she splayed them against his chest. He could feel Aimee's entire body, stiff and unyielding, against his. No doubt she was furious with him. He didn't blame her. He deserved her anger. He had acted like a caveman, and he knew it. But he had been unable to help himself. Bracing himself, Peter waited for her to push him away.

When she didn't, he slanted a look at her face. He had seldom seen Aimee speechless, but apparently she was now. Either that, or she decided he wasn't even worth a tongue-lashing.

She was right. He probably wasn't. There was no excuse for his outrageous behavior. For an astute businessman known for his coolness and levelheadedness even at the most tense and competitive auctions, he had acted like the greenest of art dealers, overreacting and overbidding.

Only Aimee wasn't some coveted piece of art. She was a flesh-and-blood woman. *His* woman. And he had been blind with jealousy when he saw her with another man.

Peter studied her face. Her cheeks had colored to a bright shade of pink. Her ghost-blue eyes were wide and filled with some unreadable emotion. The cap of dark hair on her head was tousled, as though she had just crawled from bed after a night of lovemaking—his lovemaking, Peter thought possessively.

He could feel his groin stir at the erotic images of Aimee in his bed, and he closed his eyes for a moment, battling with the need to take her here...now. Heaven help him. He had lusted after a woman before, but no woman had ever affected him like this. This constant need, this constant want. She was like an addictive drug...one he couldn't get enough of.

"Peter."

He opened his eyes at the sound of his name and stared at her Cupid's-bow mouth, bare except for a slight sheen, as though she had just licked it with her tongue. Drawing in a breath, Peter clamped down the urge to run his own tongue over those lips.

"Peter." She whispered his name a second time, and touched his jaw, her eyes questioning.

Her gentle touch was his undoing. He covered her mouth with his own. Reining in the fierce hunger inside him, slowly Peter traced the shape of her lips, savored the feel of their softness. When she parted them and eased her arms around his neck, Peter moaned and deepened the kiss.

With her back still pressed against the door, he dropped one of the hands that had imprisoned her and cupped her breast. He filled his palm with her fullness, then circled the nipple with his thumb.

Aimee moaned and thrust her body closer. Peter shifted, the ache inside him growing painful. Cupping her buttocks with both hands, Peter lifted her, pressing his hardness into the soft warmth of her thighs.

Aimee gasped, and he took possession of her mouth again. He knew he should stop. He was dangerously close to taking her, here and now, standing up pressed against the door of her apartment. The French doors that Aimee had left unfettered by curtains also left them in full view of anyone who happened to walk out onto the balcony of the building across the street.

Sweat broke out across his brow. But this time it had nothing to do with the summer heat and everything to do with Aimee.

He should at least carry her into the bedroom, Peter told himself. Pressing himself against her, he trembled with the intensity of his desire for her. Intent on taking her to the bedroom, he released her buttocks and allowed her to slide down him, to feel his pulsing need.

But Aimee chose that moment to unfasten the buttons of his shirt. She pressed her mouth to his chest.

Any thoughts of waiting until they got to the bedroom were abandoned. He knew he would never make it that far. His throat felt dry, parched, as though he had been wandering in the desert.

Aimee was a glass of cool, welcome water, and he drank from her, soothing his unquenchable thirst. He dropped to his knees in front of her and gently he kissed the inch of pale skin exposed by the cropped T-shirt.

She curled her fingers into his shoulders, digging into the skin covered by his shirt. The bite of her nails in his flesh only fed the hunger raging inside him.

Unbuttoning the snap of her shorts, Peter stroked her skin with his tongue. He dipped lower and thrust inside the sensitive indentation of her navel.

"Peter—" she gasped his name.

Holding her hips, he continued to feast on her with his tongue. He felt the tremor go through her, and groaned. His own body trembled as Aimee, her fingers locked in his hair, urged him to his feet.

She looked at him out of pale eyes that were hot and soft and filled with passion. She pulled his shirt free, spread her fingers against his skin, then moved lower and stroked his hard length.

Peter groaned as her touch brought both pleasure and pain. Capturing her mouth again, he kissed her. Fiercely. Savagely. His heart pounded in his chest, the beat echoing the fire blazing wildly inside him.

As Aimee reached for his belt, he heard a sharp rapping against the door, followed by a pounding.

"Aimee?" The doorknob rattled. "Oh, for heaven's sake, Aimee! Why is the door locked?" The knob twisted impatiently, and then the pounding started again. "Come on, Aimee. Open up! You've got to get downstairs right away. There's a guy in the shop that Jacques says is an art dealer, and he's asking about one of your paintings!"

Three

_____

"Aimee, did you hear me?" Liza gave the doorknob another twist. "There's an art dealer downstairs asking about your work. You need to get down there before that Neanderthal Jacques scares him off." Liza pounded on the door once more. "Aimee!"

"Aren't you going to answer her?" Peter whispered, his mouth mere inches from her ear.

Aimee shook her head. With her senses still clouded, her body throbbing, Aimee didn't think she could speak if her life depended on it. Though Peter's body remained pressed against hers and she could still feel his arousal, Aimee could already feel his withdrawal.

"I know you're in there, Aimee Lawrence, and I am not going to allow you to throw away this opportunity."

Peter took a deep breath. The action expanded his chest, pushing the hard expanse of muscles against her breasts. Aimee bit back a moan as she felt herself respond to him.

"You've got five minutes. If you're not downstairs by then, I'm coming back with my key. And so help me, beast

or no beast, I'll drag you out of there. I mean it, Aimee,"
Liza threatened. She gave the doorknob another shake. "I
refuse to let you blow what could be your big break for some
scheming opportunist who can't see past the bulge in his
pants."

Cursing, Peter jerked away from Aimee as though he'd
been slapped.

Her pulse still pounding furiously, Aimee barely regis-
tered Liza's retreating footsteps or her threat to return with
a key. But there was no mistaking the insult—or Peter's reaction to it.

Following Peter's lead, Aimee took a deep, measured
breath of her own. She leaned against the door, her senses
still reeling, her body weak with desire brought to a fever
pitch, only to be left hanging. Silently she damned her
friend's timing and her acid tongue.

She eyed Peter as he straightened his shirt and rebuckled
his belt, both envying and resenting him for his ability to
reassert control over his senses so easily.

She, unfortunately, didn't possess such recuperative abil-
ities—especially not where Peter was concerned. Nor was
she as adept as he was at shutting off her feelings.

And that was the problem, Aimee admitted, frowning.
Her emotions were involved. Her affair with Peter wasn't
based on simple lust. She was in love with him. That was
why her response to him was always so powerful, so all-
consuming. It wasn't simply her body that responded to his
touch, but her heart, as well.

Surely Peter felt something for her, something that went
beyond the physical chemistry they shared. She refused to
believe that he could hold her, touch her, make love to her,
as he did without some part of his heart being involved.

At least that was what she had told herself. She had also
told the same thing to Liza when the other woman questioned her wisdom in engaging in an affair with Peter.

True, he was a bit jaded when it came to love. But it was
the failure of his first marriage that caused him to be so
skeptical. The scars evidently ran very deep. He was scared,

even cynical, where marriage was concerned, and perhaps even a bit paranoid about divorce and its aftermath. That was why he had insisted on the prenuptial agreement. He truly believed divorce was inevitable.

She believed no such thing. That was why she had refused to sign the dumb thing—not because she gave a lick about his money, property settlements or alimony.

She didn't. Those were *things*. They meant nothing to her. But Peter meant everything. It was him she cared about. It was him she loved. Not his gallery or his stock portfolio.

Aimee sighed. All he needed was time, and her love, to heal him. That was why she had suggested they have an affair. But, Lord, when was the man going to realize she really *did* love him? And when was he going to open his eyes and realize that his feelings for her ran deeper than lust?

And what if he never does? What if lust is all he does feel for you?

The questions sprang from somewhere buried deep inside her. From the same place that made her wonder sometimes whether she possessed any real talent, whether she deserved to call herself an artist.

Aimee gave herself a mental shake, dismissing the negative thoughts. Think positive, she told herself. She had to envision Peter falling in love with her the same way she envisioned her discovery as an artist. Both would happen, as long as she believed they would. That was the key. She had to believe Peter would fall in love with her, just as she had fallen in love with him.

She studied Peter as he adjusted the collar of his shirt. His handsome face was inscrutable, and his deep blue eyes were hooded. He seemed so cool, so remote. He certainly bore no resemblance to a man in love. A man with secrets, Liza had called him. Looking at him now, Aimee could easily believe he did have secrets—secrets he would be unwilling to share.

A flicker of doubt shimmied down her spine, making Aimee's stomach knot. Could Liza be right? In addition to bedding her, was Peter also after something else?

No! Aimee shoved the thought aside. But as she refastened the snap of her shorts and straightened her clothes, Liza's words came back to haunt her....

The beast definitely has the hots for you, kiddo. No question about that. The only time the guy ever comes close to losing some of that cool control of his is when he's around you."

"You mean when you provoke him," Aimee had countered. "And stop calling him a beast."

Liza had shrugged one elegant shoulder. "Just remember, lust isn't love. I should know. And if I were you, I'd ask myself why he's so anxious to get married, if he doesn't believe it's going to work. Men like Gallagher don't marry a woman just to bed her. Hell, they don't even allow themselves to fall in lust with a woman without a motive."

Although she had argued with Liza that Peter's marriage proposal stemmed from some deeper, nobler feelings, Aimee was beginning to wonder. While she had never questioned his passion—he had always given himself generously and skillfully as a lover, making sure of her pleasure before taking his own—she had sensed for some time that he held a piece of himself back. That even while he was buried deep inside her, following her over the edge as they both shuddered in climax, he somehow still managed to maintain a measure of control over his emotions.

A dismaying thought, she decided, especially when she considered how completely she seemed to lose her own control while in his arms.

Aimee watched as Peter smoothed back his hair. Judging from his shuttered expression, she would be hard-pressed to say that Peter even felt lust for her at the moment, let alone love. He certainly didn't look like a man who had been so overcome by his passion for her a few moments ago that he was on the verge of making love to her standing up and pressed against the door of her apartment.

Heat, sweet and warm, wrapped itself around her as Aimee recalled the fierce need she'd tasted in his kiss, the savage hunger she had seen in his blue eyes.

She swallowed hard, trying to banish the sensual images from her thoughts. Her body felt taut, achy. Even the thought of Peter's lovemaking had her body responding effortlessly, like a priceless Stradivarius in the hands of a master musician. Of course, her physical response was all tangled up with her love for him.

The problem was, she really wasn't sure whether Peter loved her. Even more disconcerting was wondering if he ever would. For the first time since she had embarked on her madcap plan to restore Peter's faith in love, Aimee wondered if she had made a mistake. Had she been deluding herself by thinking Peter's feelings for her ran deeper than mere lust?

She cut another glance to Peter's face. The mouth that had given and taken so greedily only moments before was drawn into a frown. The line of his jaw was rigid, and his eyes were cool.

Recalling the fire in his eyes when he had attempted to punch Jacques over the other man's innocent, though misconstrued, comment, Aimee could have sworn some deeper emotion had been at work. Maybe not love—at least not yet—but surely something close to it.

What else would explain that so un-Peter-like response? A smile tugged at her lips. Even Liza had been taken aback by Peter's reaction to Jacques. The knot in Aimee's stomach unfurled. Some of the tension eased from her body as her spirits and hopes lifted.

Peter looked at her then, his eyes narrowing. "Something funny?" he asked, his gravelly voice breaking the silence. His brow furrowed. It was a gesture Aimee had come to recognize as something he did when he was annoyed.

She smiled more widely, foolishly pleased that she had not been the only one disappointed by the interruption. "Oh, I was just wondering what Liza would have done if she had showed up five minutes later and the door had been unlocked, the way it usually is."

"She'd probably have grabbed the first sharp object she could lay her hands on, preferably a sword, and run me through with it."

Aimee laughed. "Don't be absurd. Liza would never do such a thing."

"Don't bet on it. The woman's never made a secret of the fact that she doesn't like me. I guess I should take some consolation in the fact that she doesn't seem to like your friend Jacques, either."

Aimee couldn't argue with that. It was true. Liza didn't like Peter and, evidently, she didn't care for Jacques. In truth, Liza didn't like most men, nor did she trust any of them. And with reason. "She just doesn't want to see me get hurt," Aimee said defensively.

"What makes her think I'd hurt you?"

Aimee shrugged. "She knows how I feel about you. She also knows those feelings aren't reciprocated."

A tortured expression crossed his face. He rubbed the back of his neck. "I wish I were capable of more, Aimee. But I'm not. I want you more than I've ever wanted any other woman in my life, but I'm not capable of love. I've never pretended that I am. My ex-wife used to say it wasn't a part of my genetic makeup. I guess she was right." His voice grew gentle. "If it were possible, if I was capable of loving anyone, I would love you."

His words cut through her like a beam of light piercing a midnight sky. *Don't give up,* she whispered silently to herself. Peter had so much love inside him to give. She just had to keep trying to find a way to unlock the prison that held him an emotional captive.

"Please believe me. I'd never do anything to hurt you. At least not intentionally."

"I know," Aimee said, smiling. "That's what I told Liza. But for some reason, she's got this strange notion that you're after something. I mean, that you want something from me. Something besides..." Aimee hesitated. She dropped her gaze, searching for the right word to describe their lovemaking.

"Something besides sex."

Aimee wanted to cringe at the word, but instead she forced her gaze upward to meet his. "I mean something besides just a physical relationship."

"Like what?"

"Who knows? Certainly not my paintings," she said good-naturedly. "Other than my art, I don't have much else."

An odd expression crossed Peter's face, but before she could define it, he turned away. He walked over to the French doors and stared out at the street below.

"Peter?"

"You'd better go on downstairs. I could do without another verbal thrashing from your friend."

"But—"

"Go on, Aimee. You've been looking for a dealer to hook up with. Now's your chance. You've got one waiting for you downstairs." His voice was hard, almost cruel, with no trace of the gentleness of only moments before.

Aimee could almost feel the tension emanating from him. "I don't need to go," she offered.

"Of course you do." He whipped around to face her. He looked tormented, haunted, as he did when he first awoke from one of his nightmares. "Liza might be right. This could be the big break you've been waiting for."

"Then my big break can wait. If he's a legitimate dealer and really interested in my work, he'll wait for me or he'll come back. I'd rather stay with you."

"Not very smart, Aimee." He ran his finger along the line of her jaw. "We both know you'll never get that big break from me. And I certainly wouldn't expect you to pass up the chance of being discovered just for a quick tumble on the sheets with me."

Aimee gasped.

Peter knew at once that he had gone too far.

Her already pale skin had drained of color. Her ghost-blue eyes shimmered with unshed tears, then sparked with a fury that turned them an eerie silver. Her fingers curled into tight fists at her sides, and for a moment, Peter thought she was going to slap him.

For a moment, a part of him wished she would.

Feeling lower than the belly of a snake, he started to touch her. "Aimee, I'm sorry. I didn't mean—"

She slapped his hand away. "Save your apologies. I don't need them and I don't want them." She glared at him, her pale eyes glittering with anger. And pain.

Peter dropped his hand.

Shoving past him, she headed for the bedroom.

He had felt rotten deceiving her. He had seen the empathy in her eyes when he told her of his inability to offer her love. He had almost confessed the truth to her then. Hell, she'd made him wish he was capable of love. And that had made him angry.

Peter could hear the sounds from the other room. The water running in a basin, drawers opening and closing, a closet door sliding shut.

Stuffing his hands into his pants pockets, he paced the room and silently called himself all the names Aimee would never call him, simply because she was a southern woman and too much of a lady.

He deserved every one of them, and a whole lot more, for hurting her.

He hadn't meant to hurt her. He had lashed out at her because he was angry with himself—not just because he was a lying rat, but also because he was a lying rat and she trusted him. The mention of her paintings as her only asset of interest to him had been like kerosene poured on an open flame, and had brought as volatile a reaction.

The world had suddenly turned red for him. An ugly red. Reminding him of Leslie. Her ambition. Her lies. Her ultimate betrayal. The two worlds had converged for a moment, and Aimee had been the artist desperate to be discovered. It had been Aimee seducing him, persuading him to promote her career. It had been Aimee's lips whispering lies of love while she betrayed him with another man.

He'd hated her in that moment—for being an artist and hoping to be discovered—and he'd hated himself because he didn't want her to be either. What he had hated most was the fear and panic that tore through him at the realization that her discovery would probably mean the end of their relationship.

He hadn't wanted things to be over between them. Not yet. He had told himself it was because of the building. He was no closer to getting Aimee to sell it to him now than he had been six months ago. For one insane moment, he had been tempted to offer to launch Aimee, to make her into the star she longed to be. To do for her what he had done for Leslie.

It was the memory of his ex-wife that had sobered him. Realizing how close he had come to making such a mistake only fueled his anger. He had learned all too well just how cold and manipulative a woman could be—especially when the woman was an artist, an artist desperate to see her work mounted on a gallery's walls.

Aimee would be no different.

"I thought you'd be gone by now."

Peter glanced up at the doorway where she now stood. She'd washed her face, leaving the creamy skin free of makeup, her lips bare and still slightly swollen from his kisses. Her cutoffs and T-shirt had been exchanged for a sarong-style skirt and matching top in several shades of rose. The sneakers had been replaced by a pair of metallic sandals that revealed toenails painted a soft shade of red.

His gazed traveled slowly upward, taking in the shapely legs, the curve of her hips, the swell of her breasts. Desire, hot and primitive, began to stir inside him again. Clenching his jaw, Peter fought back the urge to go to her, to take her in his arms, to strip away her clothes and bury himself inside her... to reaffirm that she was still his.

"I have to go. Liza and Jacques are waiting for me." She started to walk past him.

"Aimee, wait." Peter caught her arm.

She looked at his hand encircling her wrist and then up at him. "What? And miss my big break?"

Peter flinched inwardly. He deserved that.

Aimee drew in a deep breath and then released it. Her spine was as stiff and straight as a rod of steel. He searched her face. Her pale eyes looked huge and sad. For the first time since he had known her, Aimee's eyes were devoid of laughter.

And it was his fault.

The realization made something twist painfully inside him, and he released her.

"You were right, Peter. I have been a fool. And I'd be an even bigger one if I passed up this chance. Do me a favor?"

"Anything," he said, and meant it. He would have done anything for Aimee in that moment—marry her, put every one of her paintings on display in his gallery, launch a full-scale campaign to make her a star. It would have all been worth it if he could put the laughter back in her eyes, the smile back on her lips.

"Close the door on your way out. But don't lock it. I don't have any idea what I did with my key."

And then she was gone.

And he was alone.

He listened to the sound of her sandals tapping softly on the narrow steps as she made her way down the stairway to meet the other art dealer…leaving him alone. Without her. Without the building.

He wanted to race after her.

He remained riveted to the floor instead.

It would be selfish of him to go after her. Aimee wanted love and marriage. He could offer only the latter, and then he would be doing so only because he wanted something else she possessed . . . something she did not consider an asset. The building.

Of course, he would compensate her fairly for the property when the time to divorce came. His sense of justice would demand it, even if Aimee wouldn't.

Aimee deserved someone who would really love her, not a man incapable of the most basic of emotions. He remembered seeing her with Jacques, watching the way the big Frenchman looked at her.

The memory had him gritting his teeth. Peter clenched his fists, despising the thought of Aimee—his Aimee—with any man but him.

Yes, it *would* be selfish of him to go after her.

But then, he reminded himself as he started toward the stairs, he had always been a selfish bastard.

Four

___

"**H**ere she is now," Liza announced as Aimee entered the shop. "It's about time you got here," her friend said in a whisper when she reached her side. From the tone of Liza's voice, Aimee knew the other woman was none too happy that she had not responded to her summons sooner. "I thought we should open the shop and he wandered in...."

Still smiling, Liza hooked her arm through Aimee's and ushered her toward the center of the room, where another man stood with Jacques before a series of her paintings.

The art dealer, Aimee surmised, trying to muster some enthusiasm for the man studying several of her pieces that had been displayed in the shop. Six months ago she could have done so without effort. She would have been thrilled at the prospect of a dealer showing interest in her work. Now, still stinging from Peter's words, she had to struggle for a modicum of excitement at the prospect. While she would have liked to place the blame for her lack of interest at Peter's feet, she knew the fault lay with her—for falling in love with Peter in the first place.

"For heaven's sakes, Aimee, smile," Liza commanded in a hushed whisper, nudging her gently just before they came to a stop in front of Jacques and the other gentleman.

"Miss Lawrence, I'm Stephen Edmond of Edmond's Gallery," the man said, extending his hand. "Your friend Miss O'Malley—"

"Now, Stephen. I thought we agreed on Liza."

Aimee arched her brow, surprised by her friend's behavior. In the eight months she had known Liza, never once had the other woman given the least bit of encouragement to any of the men who had come her way. Not even the most ardent or handsome of her admirers had received so much as a grin of reciprocal interest. And yet here she was, dazzling this man with her toothpaste-perfect smile.

And dazzled he was, Aimee decided. Stephen Edmond positively preened. He smoothed back a nonexistent errant strand of golden hair along his temple, with a hand that Aimee would have bet was manicured weekly. Although she wasn't a subscriber to *GQ* and wouldn't know a Versace from a K-Mart special, she would have bet her favorite paintbrush that Stephen Edmond's suit had cost him a mint.

"Liza," he continued, "has been kind enough to show me some of your work, Miss Lawrence."

"And he thinks it's wonderful. Don't you, Stephen?"

"Of course it is wonderful," Jacques proclaimed, his deep voice and accent ringing with authority. Jacques marched over to the painting she had titled *Starburst,* an explosion of gold, silver and red streaks and splatters across a canvas of black. "Any fool with eyes in his head can see Aimee's work has much passion," the Frenchman declared. "One day she will be a great artist."

Aimee's already flushed cheeks burned even hotter. What she wouldn't give for Liza's long, thick hair right now, instead of her own self-styled pixie cut, Aimee thought, embarrassed by her friends' tactics. She couldn't even bring herself to look at Stephen Edmond's face.

"How perceptive of you, Jacques," Liza quipped, her voice laced with a healthy dose of sarcasm. "Given your ego regarding your own work, I didn't think you'd be able to admit Aimee's work was better than yours."

"Ah, but I did not say it was better, *ma chère*. And now that I am to give Aimee art lessons, I will teach her how to transfer the passion inside of her to the canvas. No doubt one day she will surpass her master."

He shrugged, and the smile he gave Liza made him look like a rogue, Aimee thought, not sure whether she wanted to hug him or slug him, but grateful that he had at least stopped singing her praises to Stephen Edmond.

"But then, my true genius is not with the canvas and brush," Jacques continued. "It is with the clay. I prefer to *mold* my creations with my hands," Jacques said, gesturing with his fingers as he spoke. "Perhaps one day you will sit for me, Liza, and I will immortalize *your* beauty and fire in clay."

Liza glared at him. Tipping up her chin, she turned to Stephen Edmond. "Of course, these are only a few of Aimee's paintings. Some of her best work is still in her studio. Would you like to see them?"

"Liza..." Aimee chided her friend, embarrassed all over again. God, was her stuff that bad? That her friends had to practically force-feed this stranger with their praise? She cut a glance to Stephen Edmond, who was eyeing her paintings once again. If the man's somber expression was anything to go by, it was worse than she had feared.

What she wouldn't give for a rock to crawl under, Aimee thought. Maybe there had been more behind Peter's refusal to consider her work than his stubborn stance about not wanting to mix business with pleasure. Could it be that her work simply didn't measure up?

Recalling several pieces by Peter's former wife that she had seen at an exhibit in New York years ago, Aimee had to admit that it probably didn't.

The realization made her feel ill. Had she been fooling herself all these years, telling herself she had talent, dreaming that she could make it as an artist?

Another look at Stephen Edmond's grim expression as he continued to study each painting, and she couldn't help but think that perhaps she had.

So how could she have even hoped that Peter would take on the work of an untalented nobody, when he had once represented a star like his ex-wife?

He not only hadn't, he probably never would, Aimee admitted. Her chest ached at the admission.

And it was just as unlikely that Peter was going to fall in love with her, a voice inside her whispered. Because not only didn't she measure up as an artist in Peter's eyes, she probably didn't measure up as a woman, either.

Had she been fooling herself about Peter and his feelings for her, the same way she had been fooling herself about her art? She had told herself that it was scars from his failed marriage that had made him so wary of love. She had told herself it was his cynicism about marriage in general that had made him so insistent she sign a prenuptial agreement. Was the real reason he was so sure their marriage wouldn't last simply that he didn't love her and never would?

The ache in her chest grew even more painful. Perhaps that was why he had been able to equate their lovemaking with sex, Aimee decided. For him, that was all it had been. While for her...

Aimee swallowed past the lump that had lodged in her throat. She blinked hard, refusing to give in to the tears that threatened. She wasn't sure which was more painful—the realization that Peter didn't love her and probably never would, or letting go of her dreams of making it as an artist.

"Personally, I like Aimee's portraits best," Liza said.

The other woman's voice pulled Aimee from the bruising fog of self-discovery.

"I think one of the best things she's ever done is a piece that she gave to me," Liza continued, smiling. "It's a portrait of a young boy. If you'd like, I'd be happy to show it to you," Liza offered.

She deserved a good cry, Aimee told herself. And she intended to have one, just as soon as she ended this farce. Offering the man a smile that she was far from feeling and in no way matched the one her friend was wearing, Aimee decided to let the guy off the hook. "I'm sure Mr. Edmond's not interested in seeing any more of my work, Liza."

Stephen Edmond looked at her then out of shrewd brown eyes. "Actually, Miss Lawrence, I *would* be interested in seeing more of your work." He gazed over at the paintings again, stroking his jaw as he did so. "There's something about your style that I find quite...intriguing. I especially like the portrait you've done of the young woman. You've managed to capture her strength of spirit, while still showing her vulnerability."

"Thank you," Aimee murmured. His praise was a balm to her wounded confidence in her ability.

"I'd be interested in seeing whatever else you might like to show me, particularly more of your portrait work."

Surprised, pleased, Aimee tingled from head to toe. "You would?"

"Yes. I would," Stephen Edmond assured her, smiling. "Why don't you come by my office with your portfolio? If your other work is as good as Liza says, perhaps we can discuss placing a few pieces with my gallery. Just give my secretary a call, and she'll schedule an appointment." He handed her his business card.

"I see you're still doing your brother's legwork."

Aimee's stomach tensed at the sound of Peter's voice. She hadn't heard him enter the shop. In fact, considering her parting comments, she would have sworn he had left right after she walked out of the apartment. So why was he still here, standing in the doorway?

The smile on Stephen Edmond's face disappeared. His eyes narrowed to thin slits as Peter came into the shop and stood next to her. "William and I are equal partners, Gallagher. My brother does his own legwork."

"Sure he does."

An angry flush reddened Stephen Edmond's cheeks.

"I didn't realize Edmond's had changed their policy of requiring exclusivity rights on the works of the artists they represent," Peter said.

"You know we haven't," Edmond returned, his voice hard. He leveled his gaze on Aimee. "I didn't realize that Miss Lawrence was represented by anyone. You should have told me Gallagher's was handling your work."

"But it doesn't," Aimee advised him, confused by the undercurrents she sensed and wondering why Peter was implying otherwise. "None of my work is carried by Peter's gallery."

"Not at the moment," Peter added smoothly. "But I'm considering featuring a few of Aimee's pieces in a special exhibit."

Surprised, Aimee swung her gaze back to Peter. What was he talking about? This was twice in one day he had led someone to believe their relationship was something more than it was. First on a personal basis, by proclaiming to Jacques that they were engaged, and now on a business level, by telling Stephen Edmond that Gallagher's was considering an exhibit of her work. For reasons she couldn't even begin to fathom, Peter had deliberately misled both men. But why? she wondered, shooting Peter a questioning look. If he noted the questions in her eyes, he ignored them. His gaze remained fixed on Stephen Edmond.

Aimee studied the other man. A speculative gleam lit Edmond's eyes. He glanced at Aimee's paintings, then back to Peter. "Hoping to get lucky and discover another Leslie?"

Aimee's breath caught at the mention of Peter's ex-wife.

"Hardly," Peter said.

The coldness in his voice was like a vise around Aimee's heart, crushing her with his rejection, bringing back her earlier musings.

"As I told you, Mr. Edmond . . ." Aimee said, unable to look at Peter and see the rejection of her work in his eyes that she heard in his voice. She couldn't help wondering again if the rejection was of her as a woman, as well. "...Gallagher's does not represent me or my work."

Noting the other man's doubtful expression, Aimee explained, "My relationship with Peter has nothing to do with business. It's...it's personal."

"Ah," he said, his eyes sharpening as he looked from her to Peter. "I seem to remember your relationship with Leslie started out that way, too. Didn't it, Gallagher?"

"Aimee's not Leslie."

Edmond looked at Aimee again, then at her paintings. He shrugged. "No. Perhaps not."

Aimee winced, unexpectedly stung by the words. She couldn't help feeling that as far as Stephen Edmond was concerned, she hadn't measured up as an artist or as a woman, compared to the talented Leslie.

Did Peter feel the same way? she wondered yet again. Had he found her lacking, as Stephen Edmond obviously had? She cut a glance to Peter's face, dreading what she would see. The coldness that she had heard in his voice was there in his eyes, along with a simmering anger.

As though sensing her scrutiny, Peter shifted his gaze to hers. His expression softened, his eyes warmed with a tenderness and vulnerability that confused her.

"Still," Stephen Edmond continued, scanning her paintings once more. He tapped the edge of his chin with one finger. "There is something about her work..."

"Stephen." Liza moved beside the art dealer. "Why don't you let me show you that painting of Aimee's I was telling you about?"

"Maybe another time. I have to get back to the gallery."

"Of course," Liza murmured.

"Gallagher." He tipped his head toward Peter. Smiling, he turned his attention to Aimee. "I'd still be interested in seeing your portfolio. If you decide not to go with Gallagher's, give me a call."

Aimee blinked, more than a little shocked by the unexpected offer. "Thank you," she finally managed. "I will."

"Of course she'll call you," Liza added. Moving to Edmond's side, Liza walked him to the front of the shop, with a frowning Jacques behind them.

"Forget about him, Aimee. You don't need Stephen Edmond, or his brother," Peter told her. He scowled at the other man's retreating back. "I meant what I said. I'll put some of your paintings in Gallagher's."

Frustrated, confused, Aimee didn't know whether she wanted to kiss Peter or to strangle him. His offer was genuine, and he would honor it. Of that much, she was sure. But an hour ago she couldn't have gotten him to even look at her work. And now he was offering to place it in his gallery.

It was a moment she had dreamed of often, had wanted desperately. But now that he had offered it to her, she knew she had no choice but to refuse it. Even if she was sure Peter's offer stemmed from his belief in the quality of her work—and it was something she wasn't at all sure about—accepting it would cost her any hopes of ever winning his trust.

"I'll send someone over to pick up some of your paintings this evening and have them brought to the gallery."

Studying Peter's closed expression, Aimee silently cursed the absent Leslie for the number she had done on him. It wasn't fair, but Aimee was the one who was having to pay for the other woman's sins. But she really didn't have any other option. Because just as she knew the week wouldn't end without the city getting at least one heavy downpour to take the edge off the summer's heat, she knew Peter still didn't trust her or her love for him. Accepting his offer would only reaffirm his belief that her love was linked to what he could do for her career.

"Thanks. I appreciate the offer, but I think I'll make that appointment with Mr. Edmond." She slipped the card into the slim pocket of her skirt.

Peter blinked. "Why?"

"To discuss his gallery selling my work, of course."

"That's not necessary," he told her. His expression grew grim. "I meant what I said. Gallagher's will rep your work."

Aimee sighed. "I know. And like I said, I appreciate your offer. Really I do. But I've thought over our . . . our conversation upstairs. And . . ."

Peter winced, remembering his cruel words to her earlier, wishing he could take them back. It had been his own fears that caused him to lash out at her unfairly. He regretted what he had said. He hadn't meant to sound so cold, so unfeeling. What he regretted most was the stricken expression that had marred her face.

"You were right," Aimee continued. "It's better if we don't mix business with pleasure."

Panic shot through Peter with the swiftness of a laser. His heart began to race. Beads of cold sweat broke out across his brow. "Forget what I said. I was wrong. There's no reason we can't work together. I mean it, Aimee. We—"

"You know, Gallagher, you really are a jerk," Liza declared as she stormed over to them. "What were you trying to do? Blow Aimee's chances?"

"Liza, please . . ." Aimee began, trying to intercede.

"She's right," Jacques added, coming up behind Liza. "This Edmond fellow was interested in Aimee's work—even without Liza making the eyes at him."

"I was not making eyes at anyone," Liza insisted.

Ignoring the bickering pair, Peter focused his attention on Aimee. Frustrated, concerned, he asked, "What's going on, Aimee? You know I don't like playing games."

"I'm not the one playing games," she whispered, and started to walk away.

Peter caught her arm and turned her back to face him. "Aimee, look at me," he said. When she didn't respond, he tilted her chin up with his finger.

Her ghost-blue eyes remained devoid of laughter, and were even sadder now than when she had left the apartment. There was also a distance, a coolness, that hadn't been there earlier.

The coolness sent a shiver through him that had nothing to do with the temperature inside the shop. He sensed that Aimee was pushing him away, closing some part of herself to him...locking him out.

And it scared the hell out of him.

Peter's mouth grew suddenly dry as another surge of panic shot through him, leaving him cold...shaken... trapped in darkness. He felt the way he did after one of the nightmares, but this time it was worse.

"Aimee." Instinctively he reached for her, drawing her close, needing her nearness, her warmth, to stave off the darkness and the cold that always followed the nightmares.

Aimee resisted. She shook her head, placed both her hands against his chest, keeping him at arm's length.

Still, he didn't release her, afraid of what would happen if he did. "Aimee, please."

"Don't let him sweet-talk his way out of this one," Liza inserted. "I am not going to let you screw this up for her, Gallagher."

Peter glared at the blonde over Aimee's head.

"Do you want me to throw him out, *mon amie?*" Jacques asked.

"I wouldn't try it, if I were you," Peter warned, incensed with the Frenchman.

Aimee tensed. She pulled herself free from his grasp. "Liza. Jacques," Aimee said, her voice firm. "Please, I'd like to talk to Peter alone for a few minutes."

Liza started to protest. "But, Aimee—"

"You are sure?" Jacques asked.

Aimee nodded.

Unbidden, jealousy fired through Peter. He watched the big Frenchman's gaze shift from Aimee to him. And the look that the other man sent Peter was a definite warning. "Come along, Liza," Jacques said, nudging Liza's shoulder and urging her to leave. He paused. "You have only to call out if you need me, *mon amie.*"

"She won't need you," Peter assured him through gritted teeth. Irritated by the other man's protective instincts toward Aimee, he watched the duo leave the shop.

"All right, Peter. It's just the two of us now. So, why don't you explain to me what kind of game it is *you're* playing?"

Exasperated, Peter shoved his hand through his hair. "I'm not playing any games. I'm going to take your work on at my gallery."

"Why?"

"What do you mean, why?"

"I mean, why now? Why the sudden change of heart? A week ago, you wouldn't even look at my work. You still haven't looked at any of it. And yet you're suddenly willing to represent me?"

"Yes," Peter said, growing impatient with Aimee's insistence that he provide her with a reasonable explanation for his actions. He couldn't. Hell, how could he explain it to her, when he couldn't even explain to himself why he had made the offer?

"So, why did you change your mind?"

Peter remained silent. What could he tell her? That he hadn't wanted to rep her work because he didn't trust her? That even though he had decided to back off on his own rule about mixing business and pleasure and take her on as a client, his reasons for doing so had nothing to do with her work? He still didn't trust her not to use him. He was sure she would if he gave her the chance. But he wasn't ready to let go of her. At least not yet. Not until he got the building. And not until he sated this need for her that burned so hotly in his blood.

"I'm not buying the brooding silence, Peter. You owe me an answer."

But any answers he gave her would hurt her. And he didn't want to hurt her... not again. He didn't want to see pain mirrored in her eyes. Because it would cause her pain if he told her the truth. He didn't trust her. He would never trust her, or any woman, ever again.

"Say something," she demanded.

"What do you want me to say?"

"I want you to tell me why you changed your mind. Why now?"

"It doesn't matter."

"It does to me." Her eyes searched his for answers, answers he would not give her. "Tell me the truth, Peter. An hour ago, if I had asked you to rep my paintings at your gallery, what would your answer have been?"

"Dammit, Aimee. What difference does it—"

"What would your answer have been?"

Looking into her pale blue eyes, Peter couldn't lie to her. "No. I would have said no."

"That's what I thought."

"But it doesn't matter now. What matters is that I'm going to give you the chance you wanted. I'm going to place your work in Gallagher's." Her silence made him uneasy, caused the fears rumbling around inside him to resurface. "It's what you wanted, isn't it?"

"It's what I wanted at one time," she said softly, sadly. "Now I'm not so sure. After all, you said yourself, I'm hardly another Leslie."

He heard the hurt in her voice, and it tore at him, because he realized he had caused it. He felt like a bastard, and he could gladly have wrung Stephen Edmond's neck for his insinuations. "I would never want you to be another Leslie," he told her, pulling her close. "Never."

His ex-wife had been beautiful, talented, and as cunning as a fox. She had used him, drained him, and then dumped him as soon as a better opportunity came along.

"Then why are you willing to represent me now, when you wouldn't even consider it before?"

"Because I don't want to lose you," he admitted honestly.

She tipped her head to one side and looked up at him, her brows creasing as though she didn't understand him.

Releasing her, Peter shoved his hands through his hair. He paced up and down before her, feeling like a restless tiger.

"I want you in my life, Aimee. If it means breaking my own rule about not mixing business with pleasure to keep you there, then I'll do it."

Her continued silence unnerved him, made him edgy. Whipping around, he strode back the few feet and stopped in front of her. "Hell, if you want me to do a private showing of your paintings, then I'll do that, too," he offered, calling himself an idiot, ten times a fool, for doing so. He knew he would do it again if it meant restoring the laughter in her eyes that he had stolen. "You want a break? I'm giving it to you. If you want to be a star, I'll make you one. In exchange, you'll sign a contract granting me exclusivity on your work, and you'll give me your promise not to shut me out of your life on a personal basis until we both agree that the affair's over." He took a deep breath. "Deal?"

"Oh, Peter," she whispered. Her eyes sparkling with unshed tears, she stroked his jaw with her fingertips.

Peter shuddered beneath her touch. He pulled her to him, his mouth hovering above hers. His heart pounded an uncountable beat as his body responded to her nearness.

Desire flickered like a flame in the depths of her ghost blue eyes, and Aimee parted her lips.

It was all the encouragement he needed. God help him, Peter thought as he took her mouth hungrily. He wouldn't let her go. He couldn't let her go.

Not yet.

Not before she had agreed to sell the building to him.

And not before he had found a way to assuage this fierce hunger that only she aroused in him.

Breathless from Peter's kisses, her head spinning, her body throbbing, Aimee turned her head away before he could claim her mouth again. "Peter," she gasped when his tongue flicked the shell of her ear. "We need to talk."

"I don't want to talk. Things only get mixed up when we talk," he murmured, kissing the edge of her jaw.

She could feel herself growing weak under his relentless assault on her senses. "Fine. Then I'll talk," she managed, despite the fact that his attack had moved to the sensitive spot beneath her chin, just at the base of her neck.

"I'd rather you kissed me," he said, his voice a husky whisper.

Fighting the urge to turn her mouth to him, Aimee bit her bottom lip as his tongue traced the path where his mouth had just been. "The answer's no. No deal."

His attention moved back along her jawline, drawing dangerously close to her mouth.

"I can't accept your offer," she told him.

Peter paused, as though her words had finally penetrated.

Aimee used the opportunity to regain some control over her senses. She chanced a look at his face, watched as he struggled to free himself of the passion.

At least she never had to doubt his passion for her, Aimee told herself, seeking some consolation in that simple fact. Peter's proposal of marriage might not have been driven by his love for her, just as his offer to represent her art had not stemmed from any appreciation he had for her work, but his passion for her was genuine. Of that much she was sure.

"Use your head, Aimee. I'm offering you the chance of a lifetime. It's a great deal more than Stephen Edmond or anyone else will offer you. I meant what I said. I'll make you a star."

She offered him a smile then. "I've never wanted to be a star, Peter. Only a working artist."

"And I'm giving you the chance to be that."

"But not for the right reasons." Aimee sighed as the shuttered expression came back into his eyes. "How can you offer to represent my work, to make me a star, as you say, when you don't even believe in me or my work?"

"I don't need to believe in your work, or even like it, to make you a star."

"Maybe not. But that's what I want. Someone who thinks I have talent. Someone who sees something special in my work ... who is touched by it."

"You mean someone like Jacques?" Peter asked, an edge in his voice.

"Yes. And Liza."

"And Stephen Edmond?"

"Yes," she said, meeting the coolness in his blue eyes. "Someone like Mr. Edmond."

"You'll be making a big mistake if you sign with him, Aimee. Stephen Edmond and his brother are rich little boys whose parents left them lots of money. They like to play at being art dealers. I've known too many artists who've signed that exclusivity agreement of theirs and been burned by it."

"You're demanding that I sign one."

"Yeah. But the difference is that art is my livelihood, not a game. No matter what happens between the two of us, with me you won't have to worry that I'll cut the price on your paintings and force us both to take losses just to get even with you. I've seen Edmond nearly destroy an artist's career by driving the prices down for revenge."

Aimee could feel her fragile new confidence slip a notch at the image his words evoked. "At least he liked my work," she said defensively. "He was interested in seeing more of my paintings."

"Edmond was only interested in your paintings because he knows I'm interested in you."

"That's not true. He didn't even know I was seeing you, let alone that you'd be here."

Peter laughed. It was a short dry laugh, that held no humor. "Don't be naive, Aimee. You know how small this city can be when it comes to the personal lives of the people who live in it. Hell, the French Quarter alone is like a small city within the city. You can bet everyone, including the mimes and musicians performing for nickels and dimes around Jackson Square, know you and I've been sleeping together."

Aimee slapped him then, leaving the print of her hand along the side of his face.

Her palm stinging, she could feel tears prickling at the base of her throat as she watched Peter's eyes grow stormy.

Refusing to be intimidated, she lifted up her chin. "Maybe everyone does know about us. I certainly haven't tried to hide our affair from anyone," she informed him. "But at least Stephen Edmond wanted to represent me because he liked my work . . . and not because I was sleeping with him."

Five

"Aimee. Wait. I didn't mean—"

But it was too late. She was already flouncing off, moving toward the front of the shop in response to the chimes on the door that announced the arrival of customers.

Damn, Peter swore, cursing his stupidity. What in the hell was wrong with him? If he had thought before he spoke, he would have realized she would react as she had.

But that was the problem. Lately, where Aimee was concerned, he had been reacting first and thinking only when it was much too late.

"Jeez," he muttered, raking a hand through his hair. The day had started off bad—with the stupid nightmare again, followed by Aimee's departure from his bed—and it had gone steadily downhill from there.

If he believed in bad luck, he would have sworn someone had put a gris-gris on him. Just as quickly as the idea surfaced, Peter scoffed at the notion, refusing to give credence to the local folklore. He had heard of the talisman, of course. It was nearly impossible to live in the city and not be acquainted with the fetish that supposedly brought ill luck to its victims. The evil piece, according to local superstition, had originated during the time of Marie Laveau, a woman of Haitian descent who was renowned in New Orleans as the voodoo queen. Even though the woman and her black magic had been dead for two centuries, the stories of her powers lived on, particularly in the city's French Quarter, where she had lived and plied her trade.

Irritated, Peter shoved the foolishness aside. He paced back and forth while he waited for Aimee's customers to leave, reminding himself that he didn't believe in superstitions or in luck—good or bad. No, luck had nothing to do with the mess he found himself in.

The problem was him. For some reason, whenever he was with Aimee, he had a difficult time remembering to be logical and detached—especially when she looked at him out of those ghost-blue eyes.

While he would have liked to blame it on his hormones—because heaven knew he had never hungered for or enjoyed any woman more, in bed or out, than he did Aimee—it was more than that, he admitted. The truth was, she had gotten under his skin as no one ever had before—not even his ex-wife. And he wasn't quite sure what to do about it.

He rubbed his jaw. It was still tender and warm from the sting of her slap. Hell, he thought, working his jaw. For a little thing, she certainly packed a punch. And judging by the way she was discreetly rubbing her palm along the skirt of that sarong thing she was wearing, she had hurt herself far more than she had hurt him.

Guilt, as thick as a summer haze and as oppressive as the humidity, settled over him, replacing all traces of the irritation he had felt at Aimee's stubbornness.

Hell. He would have let her slug him again, if he'd thought it would wipe away that shock of pain he had glimpsed in her eyes before she got angry and smacked him.

Looking at the stiff line of her back as she showed the tourists a selection of feathered Mardi Gras masks, he doubted that a dozen clips to the chin would be enough to

make up for hurting her. Or that there was much chance of
her forgiving him anytime soon. He had screwed up royally
this time.

Frustrated, Peter squeezed his eyes shut a moment. He
could feel the beginnings of a headache building behind his
eyes, and he rubbed the spot along the bridge of his nose,
between his eyebrows. Opening his eyes, he considered his
situation and the two problems facing him.

His business was growing nicely, and it was long past time
to expand. Another site might work, but this was the one he
wanted, even if Aimee did refuse to sell it.

To make life even more complicated, he also wanted
Aimee. Of the two problems, wanting her was the more serious.

The businessman in him told him to cut his losses, walk
away from Aimee and the scheme to get her building—now.
He would be a fool to invest any more time in the plan. To
do so would mean risking his money, Gallagher's, and even
himself by marrying her without the prenuptial agreement.
Because she obviously wasn't going to budge on that issue.

But there was another part of him, this new, stubborn side
of him, that refused to listen to logic. And it was this new
willful side of him that had him digging in his heels and refusing to leave.

Leaning against a wall, he followed Aimee's movements
with his eyes as she led the customers to a section of the store
with framed prints of the French Quarter.

Peter sighed. For a man known for his keen negotiating
skills and his tact when dealing with the moneyed patrons of
the art world, he had exercised as much finesse in dealing
with Aimee Lawrence as a bull in a china shop. Probably
less so, he admitted.

Of course, the unexpected arrival of Stephen Edmond and
the ever-attentive Jacques hadn't helped matters. Peter
frowned, annoyed more than he wanted to be by the two
men's attention to Aimee. But what disturbed him most was
his reaction to it.

He had been jealous. Plain and simple. It was an emotion that ordinarily was foreign to him. Not even Leslie's infidelity had stirred such feelings in him. He had been angry, even hurt, but he hadn't been jealous.

Usually only a rare piece of art and the chance to acquire it fired his possessive urges. The last time he had been struck by that blinding need to claim something as his, he had gone after the pair of Rubens. Of course, he was intelligent enough to recognize that his desire for the paintings stemmed from his own sense of guilt. The Rubenses had been his father's quest—one he had had to abandon when Peter was forced to liquidate Gallagher's because of his divorce.

It was the guilt that had made him search for the paintings. When he found one, he had purchased it and then locked it away in the gallery's vault. There were those who would have said he had hidden it. Perhaps he had. He had only known that he had to keep the painting safe this time. It was as though, by hiding the painting he had lost, he could somehow hide from the fact that his father had valued it far more than he ever valued his son.

Whatever the reasons, guilt had nothing to do with the need inside him to bind Aimee to him. It didn't explain the sick feeling he had had in his gut when she walked out of the apartment. It didn't explain the hollow ache in his chest or the panic that had followed at the thought of her not coming back. It certainly didn't explain the white-hot haze of emotion that had gripped him when he saw her with Jacques or heard Stephen Edmond offer to represent her work.

No. It had been jealousy that made him stake his claim to Aimee. It had been jealousy that made him break his own ironclad rules by offering to be her patron and to make her a star.

Glancing over at the paintings Stephen Edmond had been viewing, Peter allowed himself to study Aimee's work for the first time. She had been right when she accused him of not even looking at her work. He hadn't, he admitted. He hadn't needed to. With the right backing and marketing, talent would be secondary.

He flicked his gaze over one of the abstracts. There was a raw and earthy quality to the paint strokes that he found appealing and oddly sensual. He moved on to the portrait of the woman. Stepping closer, Peter studied the painting and saw at once what Edmond had seen—what he had failed to see because of his stubbornness. She had somehow managed to capture the woman's sensuality and emotion on canvas. He examined the woman's face. She mocked him with the gentle lifting of her lips, the gleam of mischief in her eyes, and something more, something secret, elusive, yet disturbingly familiar.

They were Aimee's eyes, he realized. Only the ones staring back at him from the portrait were brown instead of ghost-blue. But the expression was the same, the one he had seen on Aimee's face many times.

The little minx, Peter thought. He felt a stirring in his loins, recognizing the look for what it was—the glow of a woman whose hungers had been sated. Aimee had painted the face of an ordinary woman, a woman who could have been anyone's mother or sister or next-door neighbor... and who had just come from her lover's arms.

With her paint and brush, Aimee had brought the woman to life. She had made her both vulnerable and strong. She had made her both saint and sinner. She had given the painting heart. She had given it soul.

He swung his gaze to the other abstract, studying the bold explosions and merging of colors. This piece, too, was evocative, caused a stirring in his lower body. He found it both appealing and disturbing at the same time.

He flipped over the price tag and smiled. He knew immediately that he could sell it for ten times the price she was asking. The businessman in him grew excited at the prospect of launching a new artist. He could make her the star she wanted to be, and Gallagher's would reap the profits. That he would lose her and her sweetness to the glitter of stardom was a given.

The selfish side of him wanted to hold her back. The realistic, reasoning portion of his brain recognized that he couldn't. He would sign her. If he didn't, Stephen Edmond or someone else would. Because eventually someone else was going to recognize the promise in her work. Even Stephen Edmond, as unskilled as he was at differentiating good art from bad, had recognized something special in the paintings. William Edmond would sign her in a heartbeat—if for no other reason than to steal her from him.

No. He wouldn't let that happen. Aimee was his. Emotion ripped through him again, with the fierceness of a hurricane. Peter forced himself to breathe slowly as the white-hot glaze of possessiveness heated his blood. The air in his lungs seemed to grow shallow. His breath hissed between his teeth as he thought of his Aimee with anyone else.

Let her go, Gallagher, the voice that evidently acted as his conscience whispered. *Forget about the building. Forget about Aimee. Let her go. You'll only hurt her.*

He squashed the voice.

He would be damned if he would forget about the building. And he would be damned if he would let Aimee go. It was too late for that, Peter admitted. He wanted the building and he wanted Aimee. He fully intended to have them both.

But on his terms. He would offer her his patronage and make her a star. And when she was ready to move on, he would buy the building from her and she would go on to enjoy being the star she longed to be.

"Quit scowling at my paintings, Peter." Aimee stepped between him and her work, as though to shield them from him. Her eyes flashing, she tipped up her chin. "Maybe you don't like my paintings, but not everyone has your discerning taste. Some people actually like my work and are willing to pay for it. I won't have you scaring off potential buyers."

Stunned by the anger behind her words, Peter blinked. "What are you talking about?"

"One of those customers was interested in seeing this painting." She pointed to the abstract he had been studying. "But she changed her mind and left when she saw you glaring at it."

"I was not glaring at it," he said, his teeth clenched as he struggled with the strong feelings still racing through him. "I was admiring it."

"Sure you were."

"I was." At her wary expression, Peter reined in his emotions, regaining control. "I really was admiring your work. Edmond was right. You are good."

"Thank you," she said, but her voice remained as wary as her expression.

"I was a fool not to have recognized it before now."

"How could you recognize it, when you've never looked at any of my work before?"

"A stupid decision on my part." He walked over to Aimee and waited for her to move away. When she didn't, he continued, "But then, it was never your work that I was interested in."

She lifted her gaze to meet his. "And now?"

"Now I want them both—you and your paintings."

Something flickered in her eyes, and then she dropped her gaze. Placing his finger beneath her chin, he forced her to look at him. "What do you want, Aimee?"

When she didn't answer, Peter said, "You know what I think? I think you want to be a star. I've never known an artist yet who didn't want to be one. I'm willing to make it happen for you. I meant what I said about Gallagher's representing you. But I want exclusivity. Everything you create will belong to me—to Gallagher's. No one but me will have the right to sell any of your work. Only me."

Aimee pulled away from him. "And I meant what I said. I don't want or need Gallagher's to act as my patron." Turning on her heel, she walked to the front of the shop.

Stifling a flash of irritation, Peter followed her, determined not to argue with her further. "Don't be a fool,

Aimee. You know this is what you want. I'm offering you the chance of a lifetime.''

She whipped around to face him. "You don't have a clue as to what I want. And you can take your chance of a lifetime and your exclusivity clauses and stuff them."

Peter sighed. "You're still angry with me."

"You're darn right I'm still angry. How dare you patronize me with your offer of representation? You make me doubt myself as an artist, make me question whether I have any talent at all."

"Aimee, I—"

"And then you insult me. You toss my love back in my face, make me feel like a harlot for giving myself to you..."

"I'm sorry. I never meant—"

"I'm not finished," she continued, poking a finger into his chest.

Her cheeks were flushed a soft rose, and her pale eyes glittered like gems. God, she was beautiful, Peter thought.

"Then you have the audacity to insinuate the only reason another dealer could be even remotely interested in my work is because I'm sleeping with you."

"I'm sorry about that, I never should—"

"And to top it off, you start talking about making me a 'star' and spouting off about exclusivity clauses on my work. Well, I've got news for you, Peter Gallagher." She jabbed him in the chest again. "I don't need you or Stephen Edmond or anybody else to sell my work."

"I know you don't. But I—"

"And as far as me being a star, if I do become one someday, it'll be because I'm a darned good artist and not because you or some other dealer decided to market me as the new darling of the art world."

"Are you finished?"

"Yes."

She started to move away, but Peter caught her arm and gently, he turned her around to face him. "You're right. You're a fine artist, Aimee, and a very talented one. And while you may not need me, I need you."

She took a deep breath and released it. "I hate it when you do that."

"Do what?"

"Make it impossible for me to stay angry with you."

The droop of her shoulders reminded him of a fierce storm whose winds had died out. He took advantage of the moment. "I'm sorry, Aimee."

"I don't want your apologies." She swiped at her eyes.

"But I need to give them." She didn't respond, simply stood stiff and unyielding before him. "I'm sorry for hurting you earlier. I never meant to, and I never meant to cheapen our lovemaking," he said softly. "My only excuse is that where you're concerned, logic and common sense seem to elude me.

"Heaven knows, I'm not an emotional man—far from it. Anyone who knows me will attest to that. But for some reason, you can make me happier and angrier, make me feel more emotions, than I ever thought possible. I don't like it. I don't like strong feelings. I never have. I've never been prone to them before. And I don't like the fact that you can make me lose control. But like it or not, you can and I do. That's what happened earlier. I felt like I was losing you, and I struck out with words... words directed at my own stupidity. Only you got caught by them instead. I'm sorry, Aimee. So very sorry."

"Peter..." she whispered. She touched the cheek that she had slapped earlier.

Peter caught her hand. He kissed her palm and drew her closer. "You could have taken a hammer to my head, and I would have deserved it. I'm sorry for hurting you, for making you doubt yourself. You're a fine artist, Aimee Lawrence. Never doubt that."

He saw the questions lingering in her eyes, the insecurity that plagued so many artists.

"It's true. You're very talented."

"Am I good enough to... to be somebody?"

"Good enough to be a star," he told her. "I can make you a star, Aimee. If you'll let me." He gathered her close, pressed her soft body against his, and some of the tightness in his chest loosened. He kissed the sensitive spot behind her ear, tasted the sweet skin along her neck that tempted him from beneath the wisps of short hair.

Her fingers flexed, her nails digging into his shoulders. Desire whipped through him with the force of a tidal wave. It was always like this with her, so quick, so unexpected. He drew a deep breath, taking in her scent—that mixture of roses, of paint, of passion, of woman. "Marry me, Aimee," he whispered.

She pulled back a fraction and looked at his face. There was a burning intensity, a pleading, in her eyes. "Why, Peter? Why do you want to marry me?"

"Because we're good together—in bed and out."

"Sex isn't a reason to get married. We both know that."

"Then what about business? Is that reason enough? I'm offering to launch your art career and make you a star."

"And what would you get out of the marriage, Peter? What's in it for you?"

"I get you in my bed every night—not just a few times a week. And my gallery gets a talented new artist."

"Who'll make you a lot of money," she added.

"Yes," he agreed. "And so will you. We'll both benefit. In the meantime, I can help you fix up the building. Maybe we'll even open another Gallagher's here." He stroked her hair, warming to the idea as the plans took shape in his mind. "It makes sense, Aimee. For both of us."

Peter could feel the deep sigh that shuddered through her, and he had to force himself not to hold her when she drew back. "What about the prenuptial agreement?"

He remained silent.

"I haven't changed my mind, Peter. I won't sign one. I can't."

"And I won't marry without one." He wouldn't argue with her again about it, he promised himself. He knew all her reasons for refusing to sign one, just as he knew his own reasons for insisting she sign it.

"So, where does that leave us?"

"I guess I'll just have to see what I can do to make you change your mind," he told her. And, somehow, he would change her mind, Peter vowed, pulling her back into his arms.

Slipping her arms around his neck, Aimee's eyes sparkled as she drew his mouth to hers. "And I yours," she whispered before touching her lips to his.

Aimee closed the door to the shop and leaned against it, sighing with relief as the air, only marginally cool, due to the air-conditioning unit's age, provided a welcome respite from the heat.

"You look beat," Liza said.

"I am. It's hot enough out there to fry eggs on the sidewalks."

"You should have taken a taxi." Flipping the shop's sign to Closed, Liza took the portfolio from Aimee's fingers and led her to the kitchenette in the back of the shop.

"Only tourists use taxis. Besides, I can't afford one." Aimee dropped into the seat and drank greedily from the glass of cold water Liza handed her. "Thanks. I'm beginning to feel human again." She leaned her head back against the cushioned chair.

"So, how'd it go?" her friend asked.

"It didn't."

"But, I thought ... I mean, you were gone so long, I assumed that Stephen and you ..."

"He changed his mind. It seems Edmond's Gallery is no longer interested in my work." Try as she might, Aimee knew she had failed to keep the bitterness out of her voice. It galled her to think that Peter had been right, that Edmond's interest in her art had been linked to her association with him. Learning that William Edmond was the man that Peter's former wife had left him for only reinforced the fact.

And it made the ugly doubts she had been harboring deep in her heart about her work gnaw at her again, like an angry dog nipping at her heels. It also made Peter's offer of representation even more difficult to ignore—especially when she knew she would have to replace the building's heating system before the cold weather set in.

"What happened?" Liza asked.

"Not much. Edmond gave my portfolio a cursory once-over, said the work was 'nice,' but it wasn't exactly what their discerning patrons were looking for."

"The pompous ass!" Liza's hands curled into fists. She paced from one end of the small kitchen to the other. "His discerning patrons wouldn't know real art if it bit them on their rear ends."

Aimee laughed. "My feelings exactly. You should have seen some of the stuff in that place he was passing off as art ... and the prices."

"Your stuff's too good for them."

"Probably," Aimee agreed.

Liza stopped pacing and turned back to Aimee. Concern etched her picture-perfect features, and Aimee wondered, not for the first time, what dark secrets made Liza hide herself away in the shop.

"Listen, if your heart's set on showing at Edmond's, let me see if there's anything I can do. Stephen's asked me to dinner."

"You agreed to go to dinner with him?"

"No, I turned him down. But I could tell him I've changed my mind. Maybe if I talked to him—"

"Thanks, pal. But I won't have you barter that gorgeous body of yours just so he'll take my work."

Liza's face went chalk-white, and Aimee realized at once that she had made a mistake. "Good Lord, Liza, what's wrong?"

"Nothing."

Aimee went over to her friend. "It was a joke, Liza. Obviously a stupid one. But I was only kidding."

"I know," Liza said, but the smile she attempted was forced, strained. She went over to the cabinet, retrieved a glass and filled it with water. After she had drained the glass, she turned back to Aimee. "So where have you been all afternoon, if you weren't at Edmond's?"

Aimee was pleased to see some color return to Liza's cheeks. "Knocking on doors, mostly." Aimee grimaced. "Sterling's has offered to take two of my paintings on consignment."

"Sterling's?" Liza repeated, obviously surprised, and, no doubt, unimpressed.

She had been unimpressed, too, Aimee admitted. Sterling's could be considered a gallery only in the most generous of terms, and it certainly wasn't of the same stature as Gallagher's or Edmond's. Not to mention that the money wasn't going to be even close to what she had hoped her paintings would bring.

"Surely you're not seriously considering their offer?"

"Actually, I am."

"But, Aimee, your work doesn't belong in a place like that. It doesn't even belong here. You're an artist. A good one. You deserve to have your paintings in a real gallery."

"I'd like to think so."

"Then why—"

"Because it's a step up from the T-shirt shops, and they're willing to buy my work. Besides, if they sell, Abner Sterling is willing to take more."

"Of course they'll sell. That's not the point."

"That *is* the point," Aimee told her. "Liza, I need the money." Aimee sighed. "Aunt Tessie may have left me this place free and clear, but the upkeep is never-ending. It's eaten into most of my savings. I've put off a number of big items, hoping that my art would take off and help pay for some of the expenses."

"It will."

"Maybe someday. But I can't count on that."

Liza's expression grew troubled. "What about the shop? I could run some specials . . . even take a cut in pay."

Aimee's heart swelled at the other woman's generosity. "The specials are a good idea, but you don't have to take a cut in salary. You can't afford it, if you want to eat. I'm not paying you hardly anything now, remember? That's why I tossed in the free rent."

"I know, but—"

"I appreciate the offer. Honestly, I do. But I'm afraid it wouldn't be enough to make a difference." Aimee stood. "I'm going to have to sell the paintings through Sterling's and take whatever they can get for them. I don't have any choice."

"Yes, you do. You could take Peter up on his offer. Let him sign you for Gallagher's."

"No. I can't do that."

"Why not?" Liza demanded.

"You know why. Because he'll think I'm using him—just like his ex-wife did."

Liza shrugged. "So what? You can't help what the man thinks, Aimee."

"Maybe not. But I can at least try to make sure he knows I'm with him because I love him, and not because it's good for my art career."

"That's the same reason you turned down his marriage proposal and his offers to help you financially with the building," Liza reminded her. "Seems to me Peter's no closer to trusting in you or declaring his love for you now than he was three months ago."

Aimee sighed. "I know."

"Face it, Aimee. Men are users. Even the ones who play the game and say they love you usually don't mean it. They all want something. Your body, your money, your soul."

Aimee stared at her friend, and was taken aback by the anguish in the other woman's eyes. Then her expression sobered, and the cool distance returned.

"Peter's not like that. He may not have told me that he loves me, but I know he's not using me."

"What do you call the affair you're having?"

"If you're referring to our . . . our physical relationship," Aimee began. Her face heated, but she met Liza's knowing gaze. "I can assure you it's not one-sided. When we make love, Peter gives as good as he gets. He's a generous lover."

"Perhaps. But the difference is, he gives you his body and you give him your heart."

The fingers squeezing Aimee's heart seemed to tighten.

"I'm sorry, Aimee. I just don't want to see you get hurt."

"I know," she said.

"I guess it's a little too late to tell you not to fall in love with the guy."

"Yes, it is."

"Then be smart about it. Take him up on his offer. Let him represent your work. That way, when the relationship's over, you'll at least have something to show for it besides a broken heart."

"You're as bad as Peter," Aimee declared, shaking her head. "Love isn't like that. Not all relationships have to end. Not all marriages have to end in a divorce court. How can you be so cynical?"

"I don't see it as cynicism."

"Realism, then," Aimee quipped. "That's what Peter calls it."

"In a woman's case, I think it has more to do with survival. And if you want to survive, you'd better get the stars out of your eyes, kiddo, and find out why Peter asked you to marry him in the first place."

"What do you mean?"

"I mean Stephen Edmond hinted that Peter's been looking for property on Royal Street to convert to a gallery for years."

"So? Peter's offered to buy the building from me any number of times."

"And you've always turned him down."

"So, you're saying that he's asked me to marry him so he can get the building?" Aimee laughed. "Liza, look at this place. While I love it, it's certainly not worth a man entering a loveless marriage for."

"Ah, but the marriage wouldn't be loveless, would it? Not where you're concerned."

"You've been watching too many bad mysteries," Aimee told her. The idea was preposterous.

"I hope you're right."

"I know I am. Peter's feelings for me, whatever they are, have nothing to do with this building."

Liza didn't argue the point, even though Aimee felt sure that she wanted to. "I don't guess there's any point in trying to convince you not to sell your paintings through Sterling's?"

Aimee pushed aside Liza's conclusions about Peter's interest in the building. "I really don't have any choice."

"Have you told Peter yet?" Liza asked.

"No."

Liza grinned. Whatever had troubled her earlier was evidently forgotten, as a glimmer of mischief danced in her green eyes. "He's not going to like it."

"No. But then, he doesn't have to like it."

"True. But he wasn't at all happy that you were keeping that appointment with Stephen."

Aimee shot her friend a stern look. "Listening at keyholes, Liza?"

"Don't have to." Liza refilled her own glass and Aimee's, then sat down. "You forget how paper-thin these walls are."

Aimee flushed, wondering what else Liza had heard. She added another slice of lemon to the water. "When I become famous and make my first million, remind me to insulate the place."

"I'll do that," Liza said, lifting her glass in a salute. "In the meantime, good luck with the beast."

"Don't call him that," Aimee responded. But even as she defended him, Aimee was already anticipating the explosion that would come when she handed him back the artist's agreement he had had delivered to her that morning.

The thought of accepting his offer had been tempting...oh, so tempting, she admitted, especially when it followed a night of the most passionate lovemaking between them. It was because she had been so tempted that she had kept the appointment with Edmond.

Edmond's rejection had stung. Unbearably so. And had made Peter's offer even more enticing. She would have signed it and accepted it then and there—even despite his cocksure attitude. But learning just how thoroughly Leslie had used him and humiliated him, and knowing that Peter believed she could do the same, had stopped her.

So she would sell her paintings to Sterling's, a fourth-rate gallery at best, which would pay her less than a fifth of what her work would bring at Gallagher's. And, with a little luck, perhaps she could prove to Peter that it was truly him she loved and to herself that she was a competent artist.

Maybe then, when he finally believed in her love for him, he would recognize that what he felt for her was much deeper than simple lust.

He loved her. It was there in his kiss, in his touch, in the dozens of flowers he had sent to her in apology over the past two weeks. She had seen it in his eyes when he looked at her, heard it in his voice when he told her he wanted her and asked her again to marry him.

But he hadn't said the words. And he hadn't budged on the issue of the prenuptial agreement. Not that the agreement itself meant anything to her. It never had. It was the lack of trust and love that it represented that she objected to.

"So, when do you plan to tell him?" Liza asked.

"Tomorrow," Aimee replied, pulling her thoughts back to the present.

"Listen, if you want to cancel the dinner and movie tonight, I'll understand. We can always make it another time."

Aimee reached over and touched her friend's hand, nervously tugging on the place mat. "I said I'd have dinner and go to the movies with you tonight."

"You don't have to. I mean, if you'd rather skip it so you can be with Peter—"

"Quit worrying about Peter. I'll see him tomorrow. I've promised to bake him some of my herb bread."

"Decided the way to the beast's heart is through his stomach, hmm?"

"Don't call him a beast," Aimee said reprovingly, hoping that her instincts were right and that she had already found her way into Peter's heart.

Six

———

Aimee dipped her brush into the paint, then carefully stroked the deep blue shade that matched Peter's eyes across the canvas. She repeated the process, applying another thin layer of color to the eyes that stared back at her from the portrait. Unhappy with the results, Aimee tossed down the brush.

"What is this? The temperamental artist is finally showing herself?" Jacques asked, his deep, booming voice and accent filling the silence in her studio.

"I guess so," Aimee replied, sighing. She wished her mood matched his jovial spirit.

Wiping his hands with a cloth, Jacques draped the figure he had been sculpting with a towel and moved the short distance from his own work to stand behind her. "What is it, *mon amie?*"

"It's no use, Jacques. I just don't think I'm cut out to be an artist. Look at this." She pointed to the portrait of Peter she had been working on for the past month.

Crossing his arms, Jacques rubbed one palm along the line of his jaw as he looked from the photograph of Peter she had propped up beside her easel to the canvas. "Your brush strokes are good, much better than your earlier attempts. The oil does not look as though you are putting it on with a mop anymore."

Aimee's lips twitched at she recalled his earlier assessment of her attempts at the glazing technique. The process was a time-consuming method by which an artist carefully and slowly created the portrait by placing layer upon layer of paint on the canvas. It was a technique used by the masters, and the end result was supposed to be a magnificent piece of art that, when properly executed, virtually made it possible to lift the completed painting from the canvas to stand on its own. Looking at the portrait of Peter, she knew that, while her technique might be perfect, she had failed to make the portrait come to life.

"It's a good likeness of your Peter. Very good, in fact. You've even caught the stubborn jaw of the man."

"But look at the eyes," she told him, frustrated that her fingers failed to create the image in her mind's eye.

"What is it I am supposed to see? They are the same eyes that are in the photograph."

"I know. But they're wrong—even in the picture," Aimee said, dismissing the framed photograph with the wave of her hand. She hadn't needed the photo of Peter to paint him. She knew his face. She knew each and every line etching the corners of his eyes from those rare moments when he laughed. She knew the slash of dark brows that made him look so fierce when he scowled. She knew the curve of his mouth that could move over her so hungrily and bring her indescribable pleasures when they made love. She knew his face, and while she might have captured the image, she had failed to capture the man.

It was the eyes. They were wrong. They held none of the compassion that was so much a part of Peter and that he tried so hard to conceal. The eyes that she had painted held none of the caring that made a man like him spend hundreds of dollars to frame a child's painting and then hang it next to a priceless work of art.

"What is wrong with the eyes? Even I, master that I am, could not have done a better job of matching the color and the shape."

"But they're not Peter's eyes. They look too... too cold. Too distant. Peter's eyes are warmer, more gentle."

Jacques chuckled. "Ah, *mon amie*, I do not think most people would describe Peter Gallagher as a warm, gentle man."

"But he is."

Jacques shrugged. "Perhaps. But I am afraid you see him in a way others do not. Of course, it is because you are in love with the man. And that is the problem."

"Why is it a problem?"

"Because it is never easy for an artist to capture the object of their passion on canvas."

"That's ridiculous. If anything, I should be inspired." And she had been. That was the reason she had decided to paint him in the first place.

"Inspired, yes. And often the results are magnificent. But the process itself can be quite frustrating." Jacques laughed again, and the sound was hearty, rich. "Just look at the portrait yourself, if you do not believe me. You see your Peter as a warm, gentle man, and you feel you have failed to capture that onto the canvas. No?"

Aimee looked at the painting. While she conceded that it was technically correct, it failed to satisfy her. "Yes."

"And while I, your teacher, tell you the work is excellent, you do not believe me. You feel you have failed."

"Yes," Aimee admitted.

"It is because you feel you cannot do justice to the original. You feel you cannot capture with the paint this wonderful person that you love."

It was exactly how she felt. "So, you're saying I should just forget about doing a portrait of Peter?"

"No. I am saying you must not paint him as you see him with your eyes, but paint him as you see him here." He brought his hand to his chest, patting the area over his heart.

Aimee looked from Jacques to the portrait. The color she had used to achieve the blue of his eyes, while correct, was too cool. She needed a touch of yellow to give the color more warmth. She turned back to Jacques. "Thank you," she whispered. Already her fingers were itching to pick up her brush, anxious to return to work.

Jacques smiled at her then. The gesture was filled with warmth, with friendship, with understanding. As though sensing her eagerness, he picked up her brush and handed it to her. "I see the muse has struck once again. Paint your Peter, Aimee. Not the one in the photograph, but the one you see in your heart."

Aimee took the brush from him. After mixing the colors, she dipped the tip of her brush into the oil and began to paint again. But this time, when she moved her brush along the canvas, she didn't hold back. Each stroke was a caress, guided by the image of the man that she saw with her heart. She painted the Peter she saw, the man with so much love locked inside him, the love that somehow, in some way, she would find a way to set free.

Her fingers moved carefully, deftly, across the canvas, and it wasn't until she sensed Jacques standing behind her once more that Aimee looked up from the portrait.

"Ah, your Peter is a lucky man. This is excellent work, Aimee. Excellent," Jacques murmured.

Aimee tilted her head to one side and surveyed her work. Her heart swelled with pride at what she had created. "It is good, isn't it?"

"It is more than good."

Aimee warmed at the praise. She arched her back, realizing her shoulders were stiff, her fingers tired. She had been working far longer than she had imagined. But time was irrelevant in light of what she had accomplished. The eyes that looked back at her now were Peter's eyes, warm and gentle, not those of a cool stranger.

Jacques was right. The painting *was* more than good, she admitted, surveying her work. It was the best thing she had ever done.

"There is only one thing you have missed," Jacques told her.

"What?"

He picked up one of her brushes, dabbed it into black paint and offered it to her.

Puzzled, Aimee took the proffered brush.

"The artist's signature." ·

Smiling, she formed the large *A* of her name, then spelled the remainder in small letters. When she would have signed her last name, Jacques stopped her.

"No," he said, stilling her movements. "You Americans. You have no sense of drama... no feel for capturing the moment. You are going to be a great artist someday, *mon amie*. Your work will require only the one name. Aimee. That should be your signature."

Holding her hand, Jacques guided the brush with a flourish in a zigzagging motion beneath her name. "There," he proclaimed. "Someday *that* signature will be a very famous one."

Tipping back her head to look at Jacques, Aimee laughed.

It was the sound of Aimee's laughter, so light and carefree, that made the tune he had been whistling fall silent on Peter's lips. He pushed the open door wider and stepped into her apartment. He smiled, pleased but not entirely sure why the mere sound of Aimee laughing could fill him with such a sense of warmth and contentment.

Probably because a few weeks ago he had been afraid he had robbed all laughter from her with a few words spoken in anger and jealousy. Thank heaven, she had forgiven him. He knew without hesitation that he would have willingly parted with his prized Matisse just to hear the sound of her laughter again.

After pushing the door closed, Peter headed for the kitchen with the bottle of champagne he had brought to celebrate. And they would be celebrating, he told himself, even as he noted the bare stove top and the cluttered table. He sniffed, then touched the oven and found it cold to the touch.

So, she had forgotten to make the herb bread she had promised him. Who could blame her? He certainly didn't. It was too hot for baking, anyway. And food was hardly what he had in mind for them.

Pulling open the cabinets, he spied the ice bucket and retrieved it from its hiding spot behind some serving bowls. After placing the bottle of Moët in the container, he filled it with ice. He settled on the wineglasses for their champagne.

Champagne. Ice. Glasses. Peter went through the mental checklist. Now all he needed was Aimee, and once she said yes, he would slip the ring on her finger—and this time it would stay there.

A surge of adrenaline shot through him. Suddenly nervous, Peter patted the pocket of his slacks, feeling for the ring. He relaxed a little when he felt the prongs of the emerald-shaped stone.

Lunch or no lunch, they would picnic here on the floor, feast on champagne and each other. He would bask in her excitement and appreciation over the contract he had sent. He would tell her of his plans for her exhibit and watch her expressive face glow with anticipation.

He smiled, already anticipating the love that would shimmer in her ghost-blue eyes when he asked her to marry him. She still wouldn't want to sign the prenuptial agreement, but somehow he would convince her.

And then Aimee would be his, and he would see Gallagher's reestablished here, in this building on Royal Street, in the place where it was meant to be.

Aimee laughed again, and Peter warmed even more to the thought of making her his wife. To hell with icing the champagne. It had been in his refrigerator before he walked over. It was cold enough. Besides, he didn't want to wait any longer. Picking up the glasses in one hand, he scooped the bottle of champagne from the bucket and started toward Aimee's studio.

"Oh, Jacques, you certainly are good for my ego," Aimee said.

"Ego has nothing to do with it."

At the sound of the other man's voice, Peter stopped, his body going cold and still as he realized who was with Aimee. With the glasses and champagne clutched tightly in his fists, he moved to the doorway of her studio.

Peter allowed his gaze to sweep over the room, barely registering the myriad of paintings lining the space—the splashes of bright colors adorning the stark white walls and filling each corner with their vibrancy. He dismissed it all. His collector's eye, an eye that had been unable to resist the quick assessment of most paintings within his peripheral vision, was unable to see anything now save the woman at the center of the collage.

Aimee. *His* Aimee. With her ghost-blue eyes bright and shining, with her soft, sweet lips smiling, with her lushly curved body encircled by the big Frenchman's arms as he held her hand and guided her brush across the canvas.

Tipping back her head, Aimee laughed again. Her face glowed as the other man murmured something to her in French.

Jealousy, fierce and ugly, churned in Peter's gut.

Damn the woman for making him feel this way. Damn her for making him want to hurl the Frenchman out the window... for making him want to haul her into his arms and claim her as his.

And it was because she made him feel those things that he forced himself to stay where he was.

A piece of ice still clinging to the champagne bottle slid down the bottle's side and fell to the wooden floor, then shattered.

Aimee started at the sound. "Peter," she said, her voice echoing her surprise.

"You did ask me to come by to have lunch. Didn't you?" Peter asked, pleased that he managed to sound so detached while the blood pumped through his veins so fiercely.

A look of dread filled her face. "Oh, my God. Please tell me you're early."

"Actually, I'm a few minutes late. I stopped to pick up some champagne," he said, lifting the bottle.

Aimee groaned. "What time is it?"

Peter tilted the empty glasses to look at his wrist. "Twelve-thirty."

She groaned again.

"It seems I'm interrupting again."

"Don't be silly." A tiny frown line creased her brow as she looked at him. "As usual, I've lost track of time." Disengaging herself from Jacques, she removed the painting she had been working on from the easel and propped it, face in, against a nearby wall.

Peter felt a swift kick to the gut at the gesture. Though he had held no interest in her work until recently and had refused her offer to view her studio in the past, suddenly he felt cheated, cut off from that which was the very essence of Aimee. He wanted to flip the painting around, to insist she share that part of herself with him.

Instead, he walked over to the worktable in the corner. Pushing aside tubes of paint and paper, he set down the bottle of champagne. "Gaston," he said, acknowledging the other man with a nod of his head.

"Hello, Gallagher. You are having a celebration?" he asked, eyeing the champagne.

Peter thought of the engagement ring in his pocket, of his plans to propose to Aimee and how he had imagined them making love in her big, soft bed once she accepted. He realized the chances of his fantasy playing out today were now slim. "As you've pointed out before, being with Aimee is reason enough to celebrate."

"Yes, it is," Jacques said, smiling.

"I take it you're still giving Aimee art lessons in lieu of paying rent." It was a statement, not a question.

Jacques's smile didn't waver, and from the mocking gleam in his eyes, Peter knew the other man had recognized the gibe, if not the warning behind it. "It's a lucrative arrangement for both of us, I think. And certainly a pleasure for me," he said. "Aimee's an excellent pupil."

"That's not what you said a few weeks ago," Aimee quipped, smiling. She stood and began to hurriedly cap the tubes of paint.

With any other woman, Peter would have suspected the scenario he had walked in on was a ploy to make him jealous. But Aimee's smile was easy, carefree, a direct opposite of the tension and envy gnawing inside him.

"You are a gifted artist, *mon amie*. I want you to be the best you can be." Jacques lifted her hand to his lips and kissed the inside of her wrist.

Aimee pushed him away and laughed. "Behave yourself, Jacques. And quit trying to live up to your reputation as a Frenchman."

Peter set down the glasses, afraid that if he didn't he would break the stems—along with the Frenchman.

"Ah, but I *am* French," Jacques reminded her.

"Yes, I know. And so does every other woman in the city of New Orleans—including Ms. Sloane." After wiping her hands on a towel, Aimee walked over to Peter and brushed her lips quickly against his. "Come on, let's see what I can do about lunch."

"Kay Sloane?" Peter asked as both he and Jacques allowed Aimee to usher them out of the studio into the apartment.

"Yes. She's hosting a special exhibit for some of Jacques's artwork. Do you know her?" Aimee asked.

"We've met at a few of the auctions in Europe." The woman was not only beautiful but loaded, and reported to have quite an appetite for men.

"Well, she's certainly pulling out all the stops with this reception she's planning for Jacques. She's hosting a little preview party for him next week. She's quite taken with his work."

And evidently quite taken with Jacques, himself, Peter surmised.

"Speaking of Kay, I must go. I am to meet her to go over a few details for the party. Kay promises the food and wine will be *magnifique* and there will be many wealthy patrons of the arts there. The two of you will come. No?"

"Of course we'll come," Aimee replied.

"Good. Then I will have at least two friendly faces there. Now, I will leave you two lovebirds to your lunch. *Au revoir,* Gallagher," he said as Aimee saw him to the door. After a nod to Peter, he turned to Aimee and kissed her on both cheeks. "*Au revoir, mon amie.* I will see you tomorrow morning, yes?"

"Yes," Aimee replied.

I will see you tomorrow morning. I will see you tomorrow morning.

The words continued to echo in Peter's head, feeding the red haze of jealousy that had him in its grip. With his hands balled into fists, Peter squeezed his eyes shut, blocking out the image of Aimee with Jacques. Jacques smiling at Aimee...kissing her cheeks...his hand guiding hers as her brush stroked the canvas...covering her fingers intimately as he would a lover's body.

"Peter?"

Peter's eyes snapped open at the sound of her voice. He stared at Aimee's face, saw the concern etched in her expression.

"Are you all right?"

"I'm fine," he lied, reining in his emotions.

"I'm sorry I forgot about lunch."

"It's no big deal." Peter walked to the door of her studio and stared into the room, breathing in the scents of linseed oil, of paint.

"My work was going well," Aimee continued. "I got caught up in the painting I was working on, and the time just sort of slipped away."

And she had forgotten about him. The realization caused an ache in his chest that Peter didn't understand. Trying to assuage his sense of uneasiness, Peter asked, "Why don't you let me take a look at what you're working on? Maybe I'll be able to use it in the exhibit."

"No," Aimee said quickly. "I don't think so."

"Why don't you let me be the judge of that? After all, I'm the art expert, remember?"

"I know. But this piece is private. I'm not going to sell it or put it in any exhibit. It's just for me."

Peter felt as though another door, another piece of Aimee, had been closed to him. The ache in his chest deepened, fueling his anger with himself for feeling this way, and with Aimee for making him feel.

"Quit scowling, Peter. I said I was sorry."

"I'm not scowling."

"Yes, you are." She slipped her arms around his neck and kissed him. "I really am sorry about lunch."

He was angry. He was jealous. He was hurt. And he had no intention of making love to her now...not when so many emotions were surging inside him...not when his need for her went so deep.

For the briefest of moments, he resisted her. But then she nipped his lower lip with her teeth and whispered, "Kiss me." And his control slipped. Peter pulled Aimee to him. He tangled his fingers in her hair and claimed her with his mouth.

When Aimee drew back, a few moments later, it was long before he was ready to let her go. "I think I'd better see about lunch," she said, her voice a breathless whisper.

"I'm not hungry for lunch," he told her, tasting the sweet, soft skin of her throat. His hunger for her burned like the first swallow of fine whiskey sliding down his throat. And he craved another taste. He wanted to strip away her clothes, to lay her on the floor in the pool of sunlight spilling through the windows and join his body with hers.

Aimee returned his kiss, inflicting her own sweet torture as she slowly unbuttoned his shirt, flicked her nails over his nipples.

Peter groaned. The ache in his body was painful, but the ache to hear her say she loved him was even greater. Always, in the past, his needs where a woman was concerned had been rooted in physical desire. Even his relationship with Leslie had been based on little more than lust. Oh, she had wounded his pride with her affair, and nearly cleaned him out financially in the divorce settlement, but she had never touched him emotionally. Not the way Aimee did.

And that was the problem, Peter admitted. While he wanted Aimee, with an intensity that surprised him—even worried him at times—until recently the need hadn't been an emotional one.

But as he looked at her flushed face, her slightly swollen lips, he found himself waiting for the words that would tell him that the passion between them was more than physical. And it was that need to hear her say the words, to have her tell him that she loved him, that made him pull back.

Aimee opened her eyes. The tiny line between her brows crinkled as she stared up at him.

A sharp, almost achy feeling filled his chest at the familiar expression. Automatically he smoothed his thumb along the frown line.

"Is something wrong?"

"No. Nothing's wrong. But I need to get back to the gallery." Dropping his hand, Peter stepped back, uncomfortable with these new feelings that Aimee inspired in him. He needed to treat his desire for Aimee like the acquisition of a priceless work of art, he reminded himself. No matter how much he coveted a piece, allowing himself to become emotionally involved would only drive up the price. Allowing himself to become emotionally ensnared by Aimee could prove just as costly. He had paid a hefty tab, both financially and emotionally, in his first marriage. He refused to do the same thing again.

"You're leaving? Now?"

He needed time to think, time to regroup. Peter began refastening the buttons of his shirt. "Yes. I need to get back to the gallery. I'm expecting an important shipment in from New York."

"But what about lunch? You haven't eaten yet."

"I really wasn't all that hungry," he told her. "I'll grab something later."

"But the champagne?"

"Save it. We'll open it later and celebrate, after we settle all the details about your exhibit."

"Peter, about the exhibit . . . We really need to talk about that, about the contract you sent over. I don't think it's a good idea."

"Of course it's a good idea," he said, fighting the uneasiness that had begun to stir inside him again. He felt as though he were back in the nightmare, locked in the vault, with the light growing dim. "I promised to make you a star, and the exhibit's the first step. I'm going to make all your dreams come true."

"Peter, that's what I'm trying to tell you. I don't think I want—"

He pulled her to him, kissed her long, hard, then set her away. "I've got to go. We'll talk about it tonight."

"I can't tonight."

"Why not?"

"I promised Simone I would help her repair some of the masks that were damaged a few weeks ago. That's why I suggested lunch today."

Peter bit back his disappointment. "No problem. What about tomorrow?"

"You could take me to the Art For Children's Sake fundraiser tomorrow night. A little bird told me you bought tickets." The smile she gave him was both sensuous and innocent, and held more than a trace of mischief.

"Evidently Doris needs reminding about who she works for," he told her, knowing his secretary had been the one to tell Aimee about what she perceived as his generosity. "I forgot—what time is it for?"

"Eight o'clock."

"I'll pick you up at seven. We'll have dinner first."

Aimee slipped her arms around him and kissed him gently, slowly, making his heart pound frenetically, making his body ache with need.

"Make it six-thirty," she whispered. "I'll fix dinner here instead."

"You've got yourself a date, Ms. Lawrence." He kissed her quickly and hurried out the door while he still could. And between now and tomorrow evening, he would set things in motion, work out his plan, Peter told himself.

And tomorrow night, he would make Aimee Lawrence an offer she couldn't refuse, one that would satisfy all their needs. They would both be able to sate this unquenchable passion that flared uncontrollably between them until the fire burned itself out.

And once the fire had been doused, when it was all over and done with, they would each have what they wanted—Aimee would be a star in the art world, and he would have his building back. And at long last, Gallagher's would be home.

Seven

Aimee stepped inside Peter's condo, the slim heels of her strappy red sandals sinking into the plush silver carpet. Her head was still swimming with the excitement of the evening. "Wasn't it a fabulous party?"

"Yeah. Terrific," Peter said as he shut the door and followed Aimee into the room.

Ignoring his unenthusiastic response, Aimee spun around, sending the skirt of her strapless dress into a swirl of red chiffon about her legs. She liked the feel of the fabric, enjoyed the swishing sound it made when she moved. She felt happy, alive, and more in love with Peter than ever.

Savoring the moment, she launched herself into his arms and kissed him. At the surprised look on his face, she tipped her head back and laughed. Then she kissed him again. "Well, I had a wonderful time, even if you didn't."

"Who says I didn't have a good time?"

Aimee giggled. "I do." With his hands still anchored at her waist, his body pressed so close to hers, Aimee was keenly aware of Peter's growing response to her nearness.

That she excited him so easily, so quickly, only added to the heady feeling of the moment.

"Well, you're wrong."

"Liar," Aimee countered. "You were bored stiff, and you know it."

"With the party," he told her. "But not with you. Never with you."

The solemn tone of his voice touched something deep inside her, and Aimee felt as though her chest would burst from the emotions stirring within her. She caressed his cheek. "I'm glad. I'd hate it if you found me boring."

"You? Boring? Not a chance." Turning his face, Peter brushed his lips along the palm of her hand, and Aimee shivered at the heat of his mouth, the touch of his lips on her skin.

"You make me feel a lot of things. Happy. Angry. Excited. Frustrated. Sometimes you even make me feel a little crazy. But bored? Never. Not in this lifetime." Drawing her more closely into his arms, Peter kissed her. His mouth was warm, gentle, coaxing, as he teased her lips apart with feather-light strokes of his tongue.

Aimee opened her mouth to him, wanting, needing, more. As though he understood her silent plea, Peter obliged, taking what she offered, demanding even more. Within moments, Aimee could feel herself slipping, spinning once more into the sensual storm of Peter's lovemaking. When the kiss ended, Aimee sank against him and drew a steadying breath. Curling her fingers into the sleeve of his jacket, she rested her palm against his chest. She could feel the quick beat of his heart beneath her fingertips, feel the tremor that ran through his body.

"If I'd known you would respond like this, I would have made a much bigger donation to the art fund tonight. In fact," he whispered, nuzzling the lobe of her ear, "I think I'll send them another check tomorrow morning."

Aimee laughed again. "You really are a sweet man, Peter Gallagher."

"Sweet?" Peter repeated, his voice filled with mock indignation.

"Yes, sweet." Tracing his mouth with her fingertips, she looked up into his eyes. "Go ahead and pretend to be the cold, hard businessman if you want to. But I know differently. You're really a very kind and generous man. It's part of the reason I love you."

Something flickered in his eyes a moment, and then he was grinning at her. "We've got to do something about those rose-colored glasses of yours, sweetheart. I seriously doubt that anyone else in this city would describe me as kind and generous. In fact, I'm pretty sure most people would tell you just the opposite."

"Then they'd be wrong."

Peter shook his head. The grin disappeared. "No, they wouldn't." Gently he smoothed a strand of hair behind her ear. "I'm not playing the role of a cold, hard businessman, Aimee. I *am* a cold, hard businessman," he insisted, his voice serious, his expression more somber.

"Dealing in art is a risky business. There's no room in it for sentiments or kindness—not if you want to survive. There's always someone waiting in the wings to discover the next Andy Warhol or Peter Mann before you do. And there's always the risk that just when some budding artist's work starts to take off, one of your so-called friends will steal them away before you even have a chance to recoup the time and money you invested in promoting their work."

Aimee knew without asking that he was referring to his ex-wife. She had heard the stories and rumors about Leslie's defection to Peter's competitors, just like everyone else.

"For all its beauty, art has its ugly side, too. Sometimes the dollars and cents make it ugly. Sometimes it makes me ugly—not generous and kind. If you don't believe me, just ask anyone who's ever done business with me. Ask your friend Stephen Edmond."

Aimee looked away, discomfited by the dark picture Peter painted of himself. She also didn't want to bring up the subject of Edmond's Gallery, and the sting that still lingered from their rejection of her and her work. "I don't have to ask anyone."

"Why? Because you know me so well?"

When she didn't answer, Peter eased her chin up with his finger, forcing her to look into his eyes. "Is that it? You really think you know me, Aimee?"

"Yes," she said, more confidently than she felt. She might not always understand him, but surely she knew him. How could she be so deeply in love with the man and not know him?

"I'm not one of your freeloading artist friends, Aimee. If you keep looking at me through those rose-colored glasses, you're only going to end up disappointed. And I don't want to disappoint you."

Dismissing his self-deprecating comment, Aimee said, "You won't. You couldn't. Not after what you did for that young man tonight."

"Aimee..."

She ignored the warning in his voice. "You gave the boy his dream, Peter. You gave him a chance to go to art school."

"It was a fund-raiser. Tax-deductible. Everyone who purchased tickets to the thing helped pay for him and the other kids to go to art school."

Aimee let out a long, exasperated sigh that ruffled the fringe of dark bangs across her forehead. "Why can't you just admit that you did something nice?" she demanded. "I saw you talking to that boy this evening. You know, the one whose painting got the honorable mention in the student competition, but no scholarship money to go with it. He told me you offered him an apprenticeship at the gallery."

Peter shrugged. "I needed some help."

"Umm-hmm... That's why you offered him a subsidy for art school."

"It was business."

"If you say so."

His fingers tightened around her waist. "Don't make me out to be some noble do-gooder, Aimee. I'm not. I told you,

I never do anything without a reason. Most people don't. You should remember that."

Aimee studied his hard expression and wondered, yet again, what was troubling Peter tonight. And why was he so determined that she see him in such an unflattering light?

"Besides, that kid will work twice as hard for me because I am paying for him to go to art school. That's the reason I offered him the apprenticeship—not because I'm some great philanthropist."

She hated to hear him talk about himself that way, especially when she knew that this wasn't the first time Peter had made such an offer. Only recently she had learned about the scholarship fund he had established in his father's name to benefit one of the centers for children in the arts. And hadn't he offered on more than one occasion to buy her building and relieve her of the burden its upkeep created?

"You know what I think?" Without waiting for him to answer, she continued, "I think you're a fraud, Peter Gallagher. I think you're a kind, generous man, but for some reason you don't want people to know it. Well, it's too late. Maybe you have a lot of other people fooled, but not me. I know who and what you are. I told you, it's part of the reason that I love you." And it was the reason she had been unable to stop loving him, even though she had begun to despair of ever hearing him say the same words to her.

"Have it your way, then. Just remember, everyone wants something. Everyone."

"Peter—"

"Everyone at that fund-raiser tonight wanted something. You think they were there, all decked out in their designer clothes and jewels, because they're so noble and want to help the underprivileged?"

He didn't wait for her to answer. "Maybe a few of them were. But most of them weren't. They were there because they wanted to feel good about themselves. Because they're hoping to see their pictures splashed across the pages of Nell Nolan's column in the newspaper next week, touting them as generous souls and art connoisseurs. And some of them were there for the same reason I was. Because it makes for good business. That's why I bought the tickets. That's the main reason most of those people were willing to fork over a thousand bucks a pop to sip donated champagne and eat little crab cakes.

"Even the kids there were working an angle. They wanted the rich folks to shake loose some bucks so they could go to art school. Or, better yet, come up with a deal like I offered that kid tonight—a job *and* money for art school."

"You make it all sound so cynical."

"Because life is cynical," Peter told her. "It's like I said—everyone wants something, Aimee. Everyone's working an angle."

"What about you?"

He swept his gaze along the curves of her breasts, her bare shoulders, her throat. It was like a physical caress, and Aimee's heart raced furiously. Her breath caught in her throat when his eyes finally met hers.

"Especially me," he whispered.

Feeling bold, she held his gaze steadily. "Well, since I've got designs on your body tonight, I guess I'll just have to take my chances and hope you don't take advantage of me."

An odd expression flickered across Peter's face, but Aimee dismissed it. She refused to let him dampen her spirits further. Loosening the knot of his tie, she caught the ends of the silk and used it to pull his face closer. "Besides," she murmured. "I trust you."

The blue of his eyes heated to black before he captured her face in his hands. "You shouldn't. I didn't ask for your trust. I don't want it."

"Too late. You've already got it." Still holding the tie, Aimee pulled him closer, until his mouth hovered just above her own.

"Haven't you heard anything I've been telling you?"

"Every word."

"Then you'd be a fool to trust me, or anyone."

"You know what your problem is, Peter?"

"What?"

"You talk too much. Now shut up and kiss me." Giving the tie a final tug, she pulled his mouth to hers and parted her lips.

Peter needed no further coaxing. He took her mouth with the fury of a storm. His kiss was hot, openmouthed, hungry. He pulled her body closer, pressed her against him. And this time, when he kissed her, there was no mistaking that he was a man who wanted her very much.

And there was no denying that she wanted him.

When he slipped one arm beneath her knees and lifted her, instinctively Aimee slid her arms around his neck. She held on to him, unable to speak, barely able to breathe, as he carried her to the sofa. Easing onto the couch, Peter sank back against the cushions with her in his arms.

He kissed her bare shoulder, renewing his foray on her senses as his mouth inched along the line of her throat. His breath was warm and his lips were searing as he tasted the sensitized flesh above her breasts.

"Ah, Aimee... You're like a fever in my blood. I can't ever seem to get enough of you."

Aimee quivered at the rough timbre of his voice.

He stroked her leg, sliding his fingers along her calf. "I want you so much. Too much. Sometimes it scares me just how much I want you."

And she wanted him. Aimee trembled under his touch, felt the hot, sweet ache building between her thighs. She gasped as he cupped her femininity, brushed his thumb across the thin silk that separated her flesh from him.

Lifting his head, he looked into her eyes. "And it's not just sex. I swear it's never been just sex between us."

"I know," she murmured, knowing he was apologizing once more for his cruel words and the pain they had caused her a few weeks ago. No, Aimee admitted, whatever Peter's feelings for her were, she did know that there was more, so much more, than just sex between them.

Besides, how could it be simply sex, when she was so deeply in love with him? She caressed his cheek and shivered when he kissed her palm once more.

Aimee closed her eyes as he pulled her more closely into his arms. Peter kissed her, gently, sweetly, hotly. Could any man make love to a woman as Peter was doing to her now and not have his feelings engaged?

She hoped not. She prayed not as she opened her mouth to him and felt the thrust of his tongue against her own. Because, heaven help her, she had long ago lost her heart to him, and no matter what happened, she wasn't sure it would ever belong to her again.

He crushed her to him so tightly, Aimee moaned under the pleasure and pain his weight caused her.

Peter broke free from the kiss and buried his face against her neck. "I'm sorry. I didn't mean to get so rough."

"It's okay," she said soothingly.

"No, it's not. I should have been more gentle."

"Peter—"

"I don't understand it," he said, his breathing labored, his voice gravelly. "I'm like a damn schoolboy whenever I'm with you, hardly able to wait to feel myself inside you." He took a deep breath and groaned again, crushing her more tightly to him. "Sweet heaven," he whispered harshly. "Just the thought of you getting hot and wet for me and I'm like a clumsy teenager. All I can think about is feeling you wrapped around me . . . all hot and tight and sweet. Do you have any idea how difficult it is for me not to take you right now?"

Desire licked through her with the swiftness of a flame at his impassioned response. "Then don't wait," she whispered. "Take me now."

A shudder ran through his body—or perhaps it was hers. Aimee was no longer sure. She could feel the struggle he was waging with himself, and she pressed herself more tightly to him.

"No," he finally managed. He kissed the sensitive spot behind her ear. "Not yet. I promised myself the next time we made love, I was going to take my time, make sure we enjoyed every moment. No phone calls. No irritating tenants. No interruptions."

"Is that why you were such a bear at the party tonight?"

"Yes. All I could think about was having you all to myself."

"You should have said something."

"You were having a good time. I didn't want to spoil things for you by leaving early." Peter trailed kisses along the line of her jaw, to the corner of her mouth, tempting, teasing. Just when Aimee thought she would go mad from the wanting, he pulled back.

Confused, Aimee opened her eyes and stared at his face. Her heart stopped, then started again, when she saw the raw hunger burning in his eyes.

"I want to make tonight special for you...for both of us."

Aimee pulled his teasing mouth to hers. She kissed him hungrily, urgently. Her heart swelled with her love for him as her body ached for his possession.

Peter returned her kiss, mastering her mouth and her senses with each stroke of his tongue. Slowly his mouth gentled, and he lifted his head. He looked into her eyes. "Stay with me tonight."

"I promise you I'm not going anywhere," she assured him. How could she, with her body and her heart a mass of so many longings that only he could fill? "I'm all yours for the next few hours."

"No. Not for just a few hours. I want you to spend the night. Stay with me tonight, Aimee. Please."

Something twisted inside her chest at his request. "Oh, Peter. I'd like to stay, truly I would."

"Then stay."

"I can't. I have an appointment early in the morning."

"Cancel it."

"I can't."

"Another art lesson with Jacques?" Peter asked, an edge in his voice.

She knew Peter disliked Jacques, and just the mention of the Frenchman's name seemed to irritate him, yet she refused to lie to him. There was no reason to do so. "I am meeting Jacques, but not for an art lesson. He's...he's helping me with something." Aimee touched his arm. "But that still gives us the rest of this evening." If she was home by five, she could still be ready when Jacques arrived.

"Dammit, Aimee. We're lovers. And I want... I expect more than a couple of hours squeezed in between your art lessons and your tenants," Peter told her, the anger in his voice unmistakable. The passion that had flared so quickly between them seemed to fizzle and die an even swifter death.

Aimee bit back her disappointment and felt her own temper begin to rise. "You make it sound like I have time for everyone and everything but you."

"Maybe that's because it's how I'm beginning to feel."

"But it's not true. It's just that I—" Aimee stopped. She didn't want to tell him just how tight the money had become, how much the building's upkeep and repairs were draining her. Nor did she want to tell him what meager sums her own art had generated. If she did, Peter's solution would still be the same. Marry him and let him take care of her— that is, after she signed the prenuptial agreement. And it was the prenuptial agreement that galled her. Not because of what it was, but because of what its mere existence represented.

"It's just that you what, Aimee? That maybe you're growing fond of your pal Jacques?"

"What?"

"You heard me." His voice was cold, and his eyes were even colder. "Is that why he followed you to the fund-raiser tonight?"

Aimee blinked, taken aback by his response. "Jacques didn't follow me to the fund-raiser."

"No? Then what was he doing there?"

Refusing to be intimidated, Aimee lifted her chin up a notch. "I imagine the same thing you were—making a contribution to the arts program for children and making business contacts. You know, connecting with potential buyers." Aimee sighed. "I don't know why you're so surprised that Jacques was there. You said yourself that Kay Sloane is a big patron of the arts. It stands to reason she would want to introduce Jacques around and generate some interest in him before his exhibit. Maybe she was hoping to get their pictures in Nell Nolan's column," Aimee finished, borrowing from Peter's own cynical assessment.

"And what about his interest in you? And don't tell me he's not interested, Aimee. I'm not a fool, and I'm not blind. The man may be wrestling beneath the sheets with Kay Sloane, but he's got his eyes on you."

"Jacques and Kay Sloane? You mean you think that Jacques...that he and Kay Sloane...that the two of them..."

"Are sleeping together," Peter finished for her. "If they're not, they soon will be. Kay Sloane is known to take a 'personal' interest in her male art discoveries."

"What a dreadful thing to say."

"Why? It's true."

If it was true, then... "Oh, my." Aimee frowned, wondering if she had been mistaken in thinking something might be developing between Jacques and Liza.

"Then I was right," Peter said, his voice a hoarse whisper. "You are interested in the guy."

"Don't be absurd. How could you even think such a thing?"

"Quite easily, I'm afraid."

She touched his jaw. "You're wrong. How could I be interested in Jacques, when I'm in love with you?"

He eyed her warily. His uncertainty and his longing to believe her were palpable. It touched another well of emotion deep inside Aimee, making her wish she could break down the barriers that Peter had erected around his heart.

"It's true," she told him, smoothing her fingers along his cheek. "I love you, Peter. Only you. When are you going to believe that? When are you going to start trusting me?"

"It's not you that I don't trust." He held her in the circle of his arms and searched her eyes. "Cancel the meeting with Jacques. You're a fine artist. You don't need him to give you any more lessons or pointers or whatever it is he does."

"If I were meeting him for an art lesson, I would cancel. But that's not why I'm meeting him." She paused, trying to find the right way to tell him. "He's . . . he's helping me se-lect some slides of my paintings that we took this after-noon. They're for a presentation that I'm making to Kay Sloane. Jacques asked her to use some of my work in her annual exhibit for new artists next month."

"That show is for unknown artists looking for represen-tation. I assumed when you turned down my contract you had decided to sign with Edmond."

Aimee knew very well what he had thought, and that she had never told him otherwise. The mere thought of the other dealer's rejection still stung—even after nearly two days. "I did. Or at least I had planned to. But as it turned out, Edmond's decided they didn't want me," Aimee admitted.

His expression grew even more fierce. "The man's an even bigger fool than I thought he was. Stephen and his brother never did have a lick of business sense. Obviously, they still don't."

"Thanks. I think."

"You should have come to me, told me what had hap-pened. You don't need them, Aimee. And you don't need Jacques or Kay Sloane, either. You don't need any of them. My offer still stands. The contracts are still on my desk. Just say the word, and Gallagher's will rep you. In fact, I'll even sweeten the pot. Not only will Gallagher's agree to repre-sent your work, but I'm still willing to take the building off of your hands. You and I both know the place is a money pit. And I'm tired of watching you beat your head against the wall, wearing yourself out to keep it up. Let me help you. Let me help both of us. Sell me the place."

"Peter, I've told you before, I don't *want* to sell my building."

"Fine. Don't sell it, then. Lease it to me instead."

"Lease it?"

"Yes," he said, his voice growing excited. "Lease it to me for Gallagher's. I'll be responsible for any refurbishing that needs to be done. We'll reopen the entire bottom floor as

another branch of Gallagher's. A new Gallagher's, right in
the heart of the Quarter, showcasing only new talent, spotlighting the stars of tomorrow. Spotlighting you, Aimee.

"Close your eyes and picture it. Your paintings, Aimee,
staged against the finest backdrops money can buy. Can't
you see it? All those bright colors leaping to life on the canvas, bouncing off walls of glass and chrome." He waved his
hand in front of them, drawing her into the spell.

Aimee's throat went dry. How easily she could envision
the room as he described it.

"Gallagher's presents the works of Aimee Lawrence, New
Orleans's newest and brightest star of the art world."

Aimee could feel her breath catch in her throat as he
continued to spin the dream. She wanted the dream, Aimee
admitted. She wanted to jump at the chance he was offering her, to grab it with both hands and run with it.

Was it a sin to want like this? To want something so much
you could taste it? And what would the price be? What
would it cost her to reach for the dream he offered and grab
it?

She looked into Peter's eyes, then bit down on her bottom lip until the taste of blood filled her mouth. It must be
a sin, Aimee decided. It had to be. Why else would the price
be so great? Why else would it cost her Peter?

Because that was what her dream would cost her. She
knew it in her heart. She could feel it in her soul. Any chance
she might have of him loving her would be lost to her forever if she accepted his offer now.

Peter watched the expressions flicker across her face.
While the thought of Edmond's rejection and the pain it had
caused Aimee angered him, this was indeed a stroke of luck
for him. And he would see that it proved to be a stroke of
good fortune for Aimee, as well.

He had told her the truth. She didn't need the Edmonds,
and she didn't need Kay Sloane or Jacques—not when she
had him. That she would sign with him was a given, Peter
decided. Moving closer, he whispered, "All you have to do
is say yes, Aimee."

Caught up as he was in his excitement about launching Aimee, it was several moments before he realized that Aimee had remained silent. Peter searched her face. He frowned at the troubled line forming between her brows, and wondered what had caused the pleasure he had witnessed moments ago to fade so quickly. "Aimee?"

"Oh, Peter."

At the dismay in her voice, he felt that sharp, piercing sensation in the region of his chest. It was that same feeling he had experienced when Aimee gave him back the engagement ring a few months ago. Only this time, the experience was more intense, almost painful.

Peter gave himself a mental shake and attempted to shrug off the odd mood that had beset him. He didn't like feeling this way. Nor did he understand it. Had he believed himself a man capable of love, he would have sworn he was feeling heartache. Only he didn't believe in love. In fact, he already knew he wasn't even capable of the emotion.

"Don't you see? Nothing's changed. I can't accept your offer now any more than I could a few weeks ago." Aimee eased herself from his arms.

"Why not?"

"Because if I accepted, you'd be faced with the same problem that's always stood between us. You would wonder if I was with you because I loved you or because it was good for my career."

"You're talking nonsense."

"No, I'm not. All the questions would be there, even if you never asked them. You would always wonder why I was with you. You would always be questioning my love for you."

Gripping her by the arms, Peter pulled her closer and forced her to look at him. "You want to prove you love me? Cancel the meeting with Gaston and the appointment with Kay Sloane. Sign the damned contract I offered you. It's what you wanted in the beginning, and it's still what you want. And you and I both know it."

Aimee pulled herself free. "You don't have a clue as to what I want, Peter. Jacques went out on a limb for me, setting up this meeting with Kay Sloane. I'm not going to let him down, and I'm not going to let myself down. Kay Sloane's my chance. And I want that chance."

Her rejection left a bitter taste in his mouth. Hardening his heart, Peter asked, "What about the chance I've offered you? Doesn't it mean anything to you?"

"More than you'll ever know. But I need to find out if my work's good enough, if I've got what it takes to make it as an artist. If Kay Sloane agrees to put me in her show, I'll know that I am. That I'm not just spinning myself some pipe dream about being an artist."

"And having your work carried by Gallagher's, one of the most respected art galleries in New Orleans, isn't proof enough?"

"Not when the offer's made because I'm sleeping with the owner."

Peter gritted his teeth. The line of his mouth grew even tighter. "Nothing's more important to me than Gallagher's, Aimee. I thought you knew that. I'd never trade on Gallagher's reputation just for sexual favors. Not even for you."

He watched the color rise in her cheeks, saw the spark of anger light her pale eyes. "And I'd never trade my body just to sell my work. My art means just as much to me as your gallery means to you. I'm going to make it, Peter. And without selling myself to you or anyone else to do it."

Peter saw the determination in her expression, heard the stubborn pride and ambition in her voice. "So, you *do* want to be a star, after all. At least I was right about that much."

"Yes. I guess you were."

He wasn't surprised, but he couldn't help being disappointed. There was a part of him that had wanted to believe that Aimee was different. That maybe, just maybe, she was as open and giving as she had seemed, that she hadn't been bitten by that thirst for fame. That perhaps she did love him and wasn't working an angle, like most people.

"It's nothing to be ashamed of," Aimee said defensively.

"No, it's not," Peter agreed. "I've never met an artist yet who wasn't ambitious. And, believe me, I understand better than most just how all-consuming ambition can be."

"Quit playing word games with me, Peter. I'm not your ex-wife, and I'm not some cunning female who's using people to further my career. I just want...I need to know if I'm good enough."

"I've told you, you are."

"But I've got to find that out for myself. Can you understand that?"

"Better than you think." Without offering any further explanation, Peter drew her into his arms and held her close. "Just be careful, Aimee. There are a lot of sharks in this business, and not all of them are willing to admit it, like I am."

"What do you mean?"

"I mean, ask yourself what's in this for your pal Jacques. Why's he going to so much trouble for you?"

"Because he's my friend."

"Yeah. And it snows in New Orleans in July. Grow up, Aimee. How many artists do you know that would go out of their way to help another artist sell her work? My guess is, not many. Face it, Jacques Gaston's out for something. My guess is, he's a con artist, and not just another stray you've picked up off the street and moved into your home."

"He is not living in my home. He's renting an apartment from me," Aimee countered.

"And what do you know about him?"

"What's there to know? He's a fellow artist and he's my friend."

"That's not much."

"It's enough." Aimee pulled away from him. "If you'll recall, six months ago I didn't know much about you either. Sometimes I'm still not sure I know you."

"That's not what you were saying a little while ago. Besides, considering we're lovers, I'd say you know me pretty well. Better than most people, in fact."

"That's not what I meant, and you know it."

"What do you want, Aimee? You want me to run to you with all my problems, like those so-called friends of yours? All right, there's this artist in Chicago that's fantastic, that I know could really be somebody, but I'm having a hell of a time getting in touch with the guy, because he doesn't have a phone and he won't respond to my letters. So I have to fly to Chicago tomorrow and convince this guy to let me make him a fortune.

"And then there's the Monet that was supposed to arrive last week, the one I spent a fortune on and was convinced had been stolen, only it turns out the shipping clerk delivered it to the wrong Gallagher's and it's been sitting inside some restaurant's storeroom for the past week."

"Stop it!"

"I'm telling you my troubles, just like your pal Jacques and Liza and all the rest of them do. I thought that's what you wanted."

"That's not what I meant, and you know it," Aimee protested.

"No, I don't. What is it you want, Aimee? Tell me. What is it you want?"

"The only thing I've ever wanted from you, Peter. Your love and trust."

He felt as though she had kicked him in the gut. "Aimee, don't do this to yourself. Don't do this to us."

"Do what?"

"Ask me for more than I can give. I've never pretended to believe in love. I don't think I'm even capable of the emotion. But you mean more to me than anyone else ever has." And if he wasn't such a selfish bastard, he would let her go.

She turned away from him. "So, where do we go from here? Do we continue with our 'affair,' and with me hoping that you'll fall in love with me someday? Or do we walk away now? While I still can, and before you begin to hate me for wanting more than you're willing to give?"

Despite the fact that it was July and even the nighttime temperatures didn't drop below eighty, Peter felt a chill run through his body that touched his soul. He turned her around to face him. "I don't want it to end."

"Why? Because the sex is good between us?"

Peter shook her. "Stop it. It's more than that, and you know it. I wouldn't have asked you to marry me if it was only sex between us. I still want you to marry me."

"But first I'd have to sign the prenuptial agreement, right?"

But before he could answer, she was covering his mouth with her fingers and giving him a sad smile. "Forget I asked. Of course you want me to sign a prenuptial. Otherwise I might take you to the cleaners, the way Leslie did."

"It's a business document, Aimee. Plain and simple. You're getting yourself all worked up over it for nothing."

"But marriage isn't a business," she insisted. "My feelings for you have nothing to do with business."

"Aimee..."

Tears filled her eyes, threatening to brim over, but when he would have reached for her, Aimee held up her hand. "Let me finish," she murmured in a voice thick with emotion. "Even if I were to sign the prenuptial agreement, it wouldn't solve the basic problem between us, Peter. I'm in love with you. And while you may want me, you're not in love with me. That's why I wouldn't marry you. That's why I can't marry you."

The blood in his veins seemed to freeze at the resignation in her voice. For the first time in a long time, Peter felt frightened. Truly frightened.

She tipped up her chin and stared at him out of ghost-blue eyes. "Maybe you were right. Maybe I have been looking at things through rose-colored glasses. I've obviously been fooling myself, thinking that someday you would allow yourself to love me. Because you see, until now, I've been telling myself that the problem is not your inability to love, but your fear of it. But maybe the problem is that it's just me that you're unable to love.''

Guilt welled up and lodged in his throat like a bullet, leaving a foul and bitter taste in his mouth. His selfishness and insensitivity had hurt Aimee. Of all the people in the world, she was the one person who deserved it the least. "It's not you, Aimee," he said, his voice heavy with regret. He touched her cheek. "It's me. If I were ever capable of loving anyone, it would be you."

"I guess I should take some measure of satisfaction from that." She attempted a smile, but failed miserably.

Peter felt even more like a heel.

She picked up her purse.

"Where are you going?" Peter asked, his panic renewing. He didn't want her to go. He wasn't ready to have Aimee walk out of his life. Not yet. Not like this.

"Home. I've got a busy day tomorrow, and I need some time to think. I think best when I'm working."

"You could work here. I could set up a place for your easel in one of the spare rooms. I've been meaning to do it for a long time, anyway."

Aimee shook her head. She smiled at him again, but it wasn't one of those big smiles she usually gave him, the kind that came from deep inside her. "Thanks. But I think I'd rather go on home. I need some time alone, and I'm afraid you're a very big distraction."

Only she wouldn't be alone, Peter thought as he followed her to the door. Not in that madhouse, with tenants traipsing through her place. Not with Jacques there.

Peter had to force himself to bite back the feelings of jealousy racing through him. He wanted her to stay with him. He didn't want her to walk out the door. He was very much afraid she might not come back.

But he had never begged anyone for anything in his life. He wouldn't beg Aimee now. He paused at the door, and when she turned to look at him, he caught her fingers and squeezed them. "If I were a decent human being, I'd get out of your life. I'd let you find someone who could give you all the hearts and flowers you want. But I'm not. I'm a selfish bastard, Aimee. I always have been and I always will be.''

"You're not."

"I am. And because I am, I won't let you go. You and Gallagher's are the only two things that mean anything to me. I want...I need you in my life, Aimee. I won't let you go."

"Fortunately for you, I haven't quite given up on making you fall in love with me yet."

And he hadn't given up on making her his wife. He also hadn't given up the idea of reclaiming his building. Somehow, some way, he intended to have them both. Even if it meant risking Gallagher's to get them.

Eight

"Here you go, missy."

Aimee held out her hand as Abner Sterling counted out the bills. "I can't believe they sold so quickly. The other one took almost three weeks to sell. Do you know who he was? The man who bought my paintings?"

"Same fella who bought the other one."

"Yes, I know that's what you said. But didn't he give you his name?" Aimee asked, still stunned by her good fortune.

"Didn't say, and I didn't ask."

"What about his check, or a credit-card receipt? His name would be on there." Giving Abner Sterling some of her paintings to sell on consignment had been a long shot at best. She had made the decision to do so more out of desperation than anything. In fact, it was only one step above propping them up along the sidewalks around Jackson Square and trying to sell them to the tourists. And the only reason she had gone to Sterling's instead of the square was that she couldn't afford the permit she would need to purchase in order to pander her art.

But three sales inside of two weeks, Aimee thought, wanting to squeal with delight. She could hardly believe her luck. It had to be a sign. It simply had to be.

"Didn't use a check or credit card. Paid cash."

"Oh," Aimee replied, disappointed at not discovering who the unknown angel was who had bought her paintings. She would have liked to know, if for no other reason than to send a silent prayer of thanks to him.

"My guess is, he's some sort of collector... had the look of somebody who knows art. He certainly seemed to like your pictures. Didn't even squabble with me over the price. Paid the full amount. And I have to tell you, missy, I thought you was asking too much for them."

"I know." She had asked for little more than she needed to recoup the cost of her paints and framing. Considering the hours she had spent on the paintings, she probably had priced herself below minimum wage. But it didn't matter. She had sold two more of her paintings and had enough money to handle the heating repairs. "Thanks again, Mr. Sterling." Giving the crusty old fellow a big smile, she slipped the bills into the pocket of her shorts and headed for the door.

"Got any more of those paintings you want me to sell for you?" he called out to her from behind the cluttered countertop. "I got enough space to take maybe one or two more of them. I'll even put them in the window for you."

Aimee grinned at the old codger as she maneuvered past the bins of poster prints, recalling his initial reluctance to take her work even on a consignment basis. The tiny shop was packed to the rafters, and if he was willing to make space—even in the cramped window—he must think the paintings would sell. "I'll see what I have and get back to you," she promised before stepping outside.

The moment she left the shop, the humidity swept over her like a blanket, despite the early hour. Smiling to herself, Aimee refused to allow even the suffocating heat to dim her spirits. Nothing could. Not now. Suddenly, the world, and everything in it, seemed brighter.

Her meeting with Kay Sloane had gone well, and while no decision had been made yet as to whether she would be allowed to participate in the exhibit, Jacques was optimistic. She'd even found a tenant for the apartment vacated by Simone last week. And now the sale of two more of her paintings...

Signs. They were all signs. Good signs. The signs that had always guided her. And they were guiding her now, telling her that everything was going to be okay. Happiness bubbled inside her as she zipped down the street. True, she and Peter had seen little of each other lately, because of their schedules. But with everything else going her way, it was difficult not to believe that Peter and she would work through their problems, somehow. She had meant it when she told him that she hadn't given up on making him fall in love with her.

Maybe it was up to her to take the first step, Aimee decided. The stars were obviously aligned in her favor at this particular time. So why not now? What better time than this morning? Hugging the newfound optimism inside her, Aimee quickened her pace toward Gallagher's.

She would play hooky today, she decided. And she would convince Peter to do so, as well. Liza had already agreed to watch the shop so that she could paint. Instead of painting, she would coax Peter away from the gallery, and they could spend the day together at Gulf Shores.

Aimee tingled with excitement at the prospect of the two of them spending the day on the beach. She envisioned curling her toes in the white sand, feeling the cool water caressing her body like a lover's embrace, having Peter hold her in his arms while the Gulf breezes wafted around them and they enjoyed a golden sunset.

By the time she reached the gallery, Aimee could almost taste the salty sea air. A day away from the city and spent at the beach was just what she and Peter needed. She simply wouldn't take no for an answer.

Pushing open the door to Gallagher's, Aimee stepped inside the elegant entranceway. Cool air greeted her sun-warmed skin like a kiss, and Aimee sighed. She breathed in the clean scents and allowed her eyes to adjust to the recessed lighting used to accent the expensive paintings and sculptures. As always, the serene beauty of the room, with its damask-draped walls and marble floors, had a calming effect on her.

And made her question her own decision to turn down Peter's offer to display her work here. Not that she deserved to have her paintings displayed with such greats as Picasso, Monet and Renoir. She would never be an artist of such distinction. She knew that.

But it didn't stop her from dreaming of seeing her work displayed in such a manner, of having people look at her work and being moved by its beauty, of feeling touched by something they saw in it.

No. Her own lack of great artistic ability didn't stop her from dreaming of the stardom Peter had offered her. It didn't stop her from wanting to be more than she was.

Catching a glimpse of her own reflection in a mirrored chrome pedestal, Aimee frowned. Her faded cutoffs and T-shirt, her bare legs and sandals, were as much a contrast to the elegance of her surroundings as Gallagher's was to Sterling's, Aimee thought. Neither she nor her work belonged in a place like Gallagher's. To even consider it was a pipe dream at best.

For a brief moment, Aimee could feel her earlier optimism begin to slip. But before she could rethink her decision and the wisdom of coming to see Peter unannounced, Peter's assistant entered the room.

"Good morning, Aimee."

"Hi, Doris," Aimee replied. "The boss around?"

"In the vault," the other woman said, motioning with her head toward the back of the gallery. "Doesn't want to be disturbed. But if you ask me, I don't care how much those paintings in there are worth, the man spends way too much time in that room. It's not right for him to be locked away in there all the time by himself. It's not normal. He needs to be with people, not a bunch of paintings by dead people—no matter how expensive they are."

"Doris, is something wrong?" Aimee asked. Doris had been with Gallagher's for more than twenty years, having worked for Peter's father when he was alive, and Aimee knew the woman loved Peter like a son.

"Given the fact that he's been like a bear with a sore paw all week, I thought maybe you two had a little spat."

Aimee could feel the color rush to her cheeks, recalling how their last evening together had ended. They had argued yet again over her refusal to sign with Gallagher's. And it hadn't helped that she wouldn't even consider his offer to lease her building. When he left her apartment, she had been confused and unsure, Peter frustrated and angry. "No. Not exactly. We sort of didn't see things eye-to-eye."

Doris sniffed. "And being the pigheaded man that he is, he's obviously been hiding in that vault and sulking ever since."

Aimee grinned as she considered what Peter's reaction would be to the older woman's assessment. "Well, I'm considering kidnapping him and taking him to the beach for the day. Think he'll go for it?"

"If he doesn't, I will."

"How's his calendar look?"

"Busy. Too busy. Why don't you go on back and surprise him, while I see what I can do about rescheduling some of his appointments?"

"Thanks, Doris. You're a doll."

"No, dear. You are." Her expression grew serious. "He's a good man, Aimee. He deserves more laughter and love in his life. There's been far too little of both."

"I know," Aimee said, squeezing the other woman's hand. She would gladly give Peter all the love and laughter she had in her, Aimee thought as she headed down the hall toward the vault Peter had installed at the rear of the gallery. She only hoped her instincts were right and that Peter not only wanted and needed her love, but someday would grow to love her in return.

Her heart pounding, Aimee looked in the open door of the vault. The room was somber—all black and gray. Thick carpet in a muted shade of teal covered the floor. A single light shone over a painting of pink ballet slippers mounted on a steel wall that had been covered in dove-gray silk. Peter adjusted the frame slightly, then stood back.

A lump rose in Aimee's throat at the utter yearning in his expression. "Peter?" she finally managed.

Peter's gaze shot to the doorway. Just as she had done countless times in his dreams, Aimee stood in the doorway. The morning sunshine from the window of the outer room pooled around her, draping her in its glow. Her short dark hair framed her face. Her ghost-blue eyes gleamed like precious stones as she stared at him. She looked like an angel, Peter thought. His angel, come to rescue him from the nightmare.

"Peter?"

Peter gave himself a mental shake to clear away the image.

"You okay?" Aimee asked. Coming into the room, she stood beside him.

"Fine." He stuffed his hands into his pockets to keep from reaching for her. He felt foolish over his musings, but what disturbed him most was his utter sense of relief at seeing Aimee standing there.

She looked up at the painting he had been contemplating. "A new artist?" she asked, obviously unable to identify the painting as any valuable work that required safekeeping in the vault.

"It's one of my father's."

"I didn't know your father was an artist."

Peter shrugged. "As you can see from this, he wasn't a great one."

"Hmm... Maybe not great, but then few artists are." She cocked her head to one side as she studied the painting. "Personally, I find it quite charming."

At best, his father had been an artist of mediocre ability. Any warmth or charm his early paintings had had was lost after his parents divorced. "This was probably one of his better attempts. Those were my mother's toe shoes. He painted them shortly before they were married."

"Your mother was a ballerina?"

Peter nodded. "I'm told she was quite good, and would have eventually become a prima ballerina, had she not married my father and had me."

"You've never spoken of your mother before."

"No reason to. I don't remember much about her. She and my father divorced when I was three. She remarried some moneyed count and moved to Europe. She was killed in a skiing accident when I was ten." But he had lost his mother long before her death. He had lost her somewhere in the heated arguments between his parents over the career she had given up for a man with no talent and a son who hadn't been planned and didn't fit into either of their life-styles. He had felt her emotional desertion long before she left them physically.

"How awful," Aimee replied, touching his arm. "I'm so sorry."

"Don't be. We weren't close. I hardly remember her." And what few good memories he retained of his mother had eventually been replaced by his father's bitter ones.

"I know, but still . . . She was your mother. No wonder you put this painting in here." Her gaze drifted to the painting again. "It must mean a great deal to you."

He shrugged. Except for Gallagher's, it was the only thing he had left of his parents. "I know it's not great art, but whenever I open the new Gallagher's, I plan to hang it in the section featuring local artists. Somehow I thought my father might like that."

Aimee's fingers tightened on his sleeve. "What a lovely idea. I'm sure your father would be very pleased."

Embarrassed by his own sentimentality, and Aimee's ability to recognize it, Peter changed the subject. "So what brings you here? I thought you had another art lesson with Jacques this morning."

"I did. But I decided to cancel it and pay you a visit instead."

Peter grinned, both surprised and pleased.

"Wipe that smile off your face, Peter Gallagher."

"Why? I've always thought Gaston's art lessons were a waste of your time, anyway, not to mention a convenient means to avoid paying rent."

"I refuse to discuss Jacques with you. That's not why I'm here."

"Not that I'm complaining, or that you need any reason to visit, but was there a particular reason you came by?"

"Actually there is. I'm here to kidnap you."

"Kidnap me?"

Aimee laughed. She reached up and brushed her mouth against his. "Yes. I've decided we both deserve a day off."

"Did you now?"

"Yes, I did."

Peter pulled her more closely into his arms. "And did you have a particular way in mind for us to spend the day?" he asked, catching her festive mood.

"Umm-hmm . . . I'm taking you to the beach."

Peter paused. "The beach?"

"Gulf Shores, actually. There aren't any casinos there to block our view of the sunset." She kissed him again, then grabbed his hand and urged him toward the door.

"Aimee, as much as I'd like to, I can't just take off with you and go to Alabama."

"Of course you can."

He stood firm, drawing Aimee's progression toward the door to a halt. "I have appointments scheduled all afternoon."

"Doris is rescheduling them as we speak."

He started to object, but Aimee pressed her fingers to his lips. "You deserve some time off. We both do. Forget about the gallery and business today. Let's play hooky together."

He was probably crazy. Canceling appointments and taking off for the beach was no way to run a business. But the temptation of spending the day with Aimee was too much to resist. "All right."

Ushering her out of the vault, Peter shoved the door closed and reset the alarm code. He reached for the jacket hanging on the valet in his office.

Aimee grabbed his hand before he could retrieve it. "You won't need a jacket at the beach," she told him. "Or that blasted tie." Grinning, she reached up, unknotted his tie and pulled it from his neck. She tossed it toward the valet stand, where it struck his jacket before sliding to the floor.

Peter cocked his brow. "And just what do I need for the beach?"

"A swimsuit." She gave him another impish smile. "That is, unless you're brave enough to risk skinny-dipping with me."

As it turned out, neither of them was brave enough to risk skinny-dipping. While the idea of making love to Aimee with the sea swirling around them was a tantalizing thought, making the fantasy a reality was impossible.

The beach was everything Aimee had promised—white sand, cool, clear water and warm summer breezes. It was also packed with sun worshipers, an inordinate number of small children and parents among them, obviously trying to make the most of the final weeks of summer before the new school year began.

Lying on the beach blanket, Peter propped himself up on one elbow, with the cellular flip phone pressed to his ear, while Doris gave him a list of messages. Half listening, he watched as Aimee frolicked along the shoreline. The simple white swimsuit she wore skimmed her body, cupping the soft curves of her bottom, the lean lines of her hips and waist. The sun had painted her skin a soft creamy shade that reminded him of café au lait, the coffee-and-warm-milk favorite indigenous to the French Quarter of New Orleans. Peter could feel himself growing hard as he contemplated peeling away the straps of her suit and discovering those portions of her body that remained untouched by the sun.

"Peter." Aimee waved to him from the water's edge, beckoning him to join her.

Peter pointed to the phone in his hand. After making a face at him, she raced out into the surf and dived into the water.

"I've got a list of the flights out on Saturday," Doris said.

Several seconds passed, and Peter sat up, his heart beating anxiously as he waited for Aimee to resurface. When her dark head broke the water, he released a breath he hadn't even realized he was holding.

"Peter? Peter, are you there?"

"Sorry, Doris. What was that you said?"

"I asked if you wanted me to go over the flight schedules to Chicago with you."

"When does Hendrickson want to meet?"

"On Saturday. There's a flight that leaves at nine-thirty in the morning and puts you into Chicago at . . ."

The rest of Doris's words were lost as he watched Aimee emerge from the water and start toward the shore. Her white swimsuit was plastered against her body, and her skin glistened as water streamed in tiny rivulets down her throat, between her breasts. She looked like a sea nymph, Peter thought as she raced from the shore toward him.

Laughing, she dropped to her knees onto the blanket in front of him and grabbed the cellular phone from his fingers. "I'm sorry, but Mr. Gallagher's been called away on an urgent matter. He'll have to call you back." She pressed the off button and tossed the phone into the sand.

"An urgent matter?" Peter repeated.

"A most urgent matter," she informed him before launching herself into his arms and knocking him back onto the blanket. "Me," she whispered just before she fastened her mouth to his.

Peter closed his arms around her. He could feel the heat from her body penetrating her wet swimsuit. She shifted slightly, easing her thigh between his legs. He sucked in his breath at the movement, then groaned as she rubbed against his hardening length.

He felt the smile spread across her lips at his reaction. When she traced his mouth with her tongue, Peter's control broke. He flipped Aimee onto her back. The surprised look in her ghost-blue eyes quickly turned to one of hunger, a deep sensual hunger that resembled his own.

When he lowered his mouth to kiss her this time, there was no more teasing, no more playing, only need—a deep, powerful, all-consuming need.

Aimee opened her mouth to him. And when Peter thrust his tongue inside to mate with hers, she welcomed him as only Aimee could.

"Peter..." she murmured his name. She curled her fingers into his bare shoulders, marking his skin as she had already managed to mark his very existence, filling his thoughts with her scent, with her touch, with her laughter and image.

His heart pounded so loudly, Peter thought surely the thing would burst and he would die here on the beach—hot and heavy with his need for Aimee.

She arched her body toward him, and he shuddered. At least he would die a happy man, he mused. Surrendering to the torment of his need for her, Peter kissed Aimee again, giving into the madness that only she could make him feel.

He tore his mouth free from her lips and was about to taste the skin at her neck when he heard the first giggle.

"Mommy, come see! They're kissing!" a little boy called out.

Peter froze at the sound of the child's voice. Struggling to regain control of himself, he drew a deep breath and strained to quell the painful ache in his lower body. After a few seconds, he reluctantly lifted his head.

Opening his eyes, he looked into the face of the intruder. A young boy of about four or five sat scant inches away. The tyke was crouched on his hands and knees, his head was turned at an odd angle. He stared at Peter out of curious dark brown eyes. "Do you like kissing girls?" he asked.

"I like kissing this one," Peter said. To demonstrate, he gave Aimee a quick peck on the lips.

The boy's eyes grew even wider.

"Hi, there," Aimee said, sitting up.

"Hi," the boy said. He looked from Aimee to Peter and back again. "Are you playing mommy and daddy? Is that why you were kissing? My mommy and daddy were kissing, and now I'm going to get a baby brother. Are you going to get a baby, too?"

"So, that's how it's done," Aimee said, her lips twitching as she shot a look at Peter and then turned back to the boy.

"Yeah. My daddy said that when a mommy and daddy kiss, they—"

"Timmy? Timmy, where are you?" a young pregnant woman called from the beach.

The boy scrambled to his feet and started waving his hands. "Here I am! I'm over here, Mommy! I gotta go," he told them, and he was off, racing toward his mother, kicking up a flurry of sand that managed to scatter all over the two of them.

As Peter brushed the sand away from his face and arms, the child's words played over and over in his head. *Are you playing mommy and daddy?*

Peter stared out at the beach in the direction Timmy had gone, and for the first time in a long time, he found himself thinking about what it would be like to be a father. He had given little thought to fatherhood—at least since Leslie had confessed that the child she had been carrying wasn't his. Perhaps she had been right when she told him he was too cold to make anyone a good husband or father, that he had a calculator for a heart. He had never been a man of strong emotions. He still wasn't.

Looking at Aimee, he tried to imagine her pregnant with his child. He found the idea strangely appealing, and frightening at the same time. Peter shook his head at the notion. Even if he and Aimee were ever to marry, he had no intention of bringing a child into the world. His conscience would never sanction such a thing—not when the marriage had little chance of lasting. He had been the child of divorced parents, and he knew firsthand just how ugly and painful divorce could be for a child. He refused to put a child through the same bitter experience he had been through with his own parents.

"You okay?" Aimee asked.

"Fine," he said, but Peter was no longer sure that was true. He didn't understand the strange empty feeling inside his gut when he thought of Aimee and her never carrying his child. "We should be heading back."

"Do we have to? Couldn't we stay a little longer? At least until the sun sets?" Aimee asked.

"Sure. We'll stay until sunset."

An hour later, as they sat on the beach and watched the sun begin its descent, Aimee said, "I wish today didn't have to end."

"Me too," he told her. "But nothing lasts forever. Not even a day like this one." He brushed a strand of hair behind her ear. "We have to get back."

"I know," Aimee said, wishing they could stay here forever. The day had been a magical one for her. For Peter, too, judging from his response. She thought of how contented and relaxed he had looked when he helped her build a sand castle. When he had joined her in the surf and allowed himself to be swept to the shore on the waves. When he had kissed her so hungrily and passionately as they lay together on the beach. She had felt closer to Peter today than ever before, and because of that closeness, she had allowed herself to believe that perhaps he did love her.

She studied the distant expression on Peter's face as he instructed Doris to set up business meetings for the next morning. Peter didn't even remotely resemble a man who was in love—not when he could shut off his emotions so quickly. Aimee sighed, her heart heavy with disappointment. She had been so sure that the sale of her paintings that morning was a sign. Could she have been so wrong? Was it possible that she could fuel such passion in him and still not touch his heart?

Shaking out the blanket, Aimee watched the grains of sand scatter in the wind, taking with it the special magic that had been hers and Peter's for a short time.

"Ready?" he asked, taking the blanket and bag from her.

Aimee turned to look one last time at the beach. The sun was a glorious ball of orange and gold that filled the sky. Its rim sat poised on the edge of the water, like a gymnast on the tip of a balance beam. Then it tilted and began to slide into the darkening waters.

And as it disappeared, Aimee shuddered, unable to shake the feeling that the magical moments she had shared with Peter and her dreams of a future with him were sinking along with it.

Nine

"**D**id anyone ever tell you that these stairs are murder?" Peter asked as he followed Aimee up the steep stairway leading to her apartment.

"All the time," Aimee told him. Pushing open the door to her apartment, she dumped her bag on the floor and then flopped down on the couch. "But you have to admit, it's great exercise."

"Right." Peter put down the ice chest and beach ball he had been carrying and sat down beside her. "We made pretty good time getting back. What do you say to a quick shower and going out for a bite to eat?"

"The shower sounds good," Aimee said, noting the traces of sand that clung to her legs and feet. "But I'd rather stay here. How about if we order pizza?"

"You're the only woman I know who would turn down filet mignon for pizza." Peter walked over to the phone. "I suppose you want anchovies?"

"Definitely," she said, attempting to recapture some of her earlier optimism.

Peter made a face, then grinned. Lifting the receiver, he punched out several numbers and asked for information.

Aimee breathed easier at his shift in mood. She hadn't understood what caused Peter's earlier transformation from lighthearted to somber on the drive back. She was simply glad that whatever had been troubling him seemed to have been forgotten as they neared home.

"Aimee." The urgent calling of her name was followed by a quick rap at the door before it was pushed open. "*Mon amie,* where have you been?" Jacques asked as he came into the room. "I have been trying to reach you all afternoon."

Peter's expression hardened. He hung up the phone. "In America, it's customary for a gentleman to wait until he's been invited to enter a woman's apartment."

Jacques swung his gaze from Aimee to Peter and back again. His eyes shimmered with amusement before he turned back to Peter. "Ah, but I am no gentleman, Gallagher. And most of the ladies of my acquaintance are only too happy to issue me an invitation to enter their apartments."

Peter started toward Jacques, but Aimee stepped between the two men. "Behave yourself. Both of you." She had spent enough time with Jacques to know the Frenchman found Peter's jealousy amusing. Besides, she was fairly convinced that, whatever his relationship might be with Kay Sloane, Jacques's real interest lay with Liza. "Why were you trying to reach me?"

"Because Kay has decided to use two of your paintings in the exhibit."

Aimee's heart stopped, then started again. "Really?"

"Really." Jacques grinned. He gave her shoulder a friendly squeeze. "It's true, *mon amie.* You're going to be part of the exhibit. Not only that, but Kay is going to use one of your paintings as part of the press kit announcing the exhibit."

"I can hardly believe it." Aimee returned to the couch and sank down on the cushions, afraid her shaky legs would give out on her.

"Believe it," Jacques said. "You're on your way, *mon amie.*"

It was a dream come true. In the past, those artists whose work was a part of similar exhibits had gone on to sign with reputable galleries in New Orleans and abroad. The exhibit would open up a whole new world of possibilities for her professionally—and, with luck, financially, too.

"Congratulations, Aimee," Peter said, but his voice and expression held none of the joy she had hoped he would feel for her.

"You must call Kay right away. She is anxious to speak to you," Jacques advised her. Before she could move, he was retrieving the portable phone from the table and punching out Kay Sloane's number. "Kay, it is Jacques. Aimee wishes to speak with you."

"Hello, Ms. Sloane..."

Peter stood stiff and silent throughout her short conversation with Kay Sloane. With his arms folded over his chest, his expression grim, he looked cold and forbidding. "Yes, I understand. And thank you again."

As soon as she hit the off button on the telephone, Jacques pulled her to her feet. "This calls for a celebration," he declared as he lifted her and swung her around.

"Jacques, put me down," Aimee said, laughing at his enthusiasm.

"I have a bottle of champagne in my apartment," he said, releasing her. "I was saving it for my opening, but we will drink it tonight instead. I will retrieve it, and the hardhearted Liza, and the four of us will celebrate your success."

Aimee clutched her hand to her breast, her head swimming at the sudden turn of events. Still laughing, she cut a glance to Peter. His face was a study in sadness. He reminded her of a little boy who had just discovered that there was no Santa Claus. She had suspected for some time that her potential success as an artist made Peter feel threatened, somehow. Seeing the utter loneliness in his eyes confirmed her suspicions.

"Gallagher, you get the glasses. I will be back in a moment with the champagne and Liza."

"Jacques, wait," Aimee said, stopping him at the door. "Would you mind terribly if we held off and celebrated another time?"

"But, Aimee—"

"Please, Jacques," she said, touching his arm. "Peter and I had made plans for a quiet evening alone. We've got a pizza on the way."

Jacques rolled his eyes heavenward and muttered something in French. "As you wish, *mon amie.* But if I live to be a hundred, I don't think I will ever understand you Americans."

"You didn't have to do that for my sake," Peter said, once the door had closed behind Jacques. "You have every reason to celebrate. I'm sure you'll be a big success."

"I certainly hope so, but I'm not counting on anything." Silence hung in the room between them for long moments. Aimee willed Peter to come to her, to take her in his arms and hold her, to tell her that he was proud of her, that he loved her, to tell her that he wanted her to be a success.

But he walked over to the doors leading to the balcony and looked out at the dark street instead. When he turned back to face her, he seemed more distant than ever. Aimee's hopes plummeted. It was as though the magical afternoon at the beach had never happened.

The arrival of the pizza ten minutes later broke the brooding silence, but not the invisible wall that Peter had managed to throw up between them.

Shifting from her seat on the floor, Aimee looked across the coffee table at Peter's unsmiling face. So much for signs, she thought glumly.

Peter picked another anchovy off his slice of pizza and pushed it aside. He started to take a bite, then put it down on the paper plate. "This isn't right, Aimee. I feel like a jerk making you eat pizza tonight. Gaston at least had the right idea. You should be celebrating, and pizza just doesn't cut it, as far as I'm concerned. I know it's late, but I can probably still get us a reservation at the Grill Room. How about it?''

Aimee set down her own slice of pizza, frustrated because she had been unable to reach him. ''Thanks, but I'm really not very hungry. The truth is, I'm kind of tired. Would you mind if we just called it a night? I'll give you a call in the morning.''

Surprise flickered in his eyes, along with what appeared to be disappointment. That Peter would spend the night at her apartment had been an unspoken but foregone conclusion. ''All right, if that's what you want.''

''It is.''

Pushing away from the table, Peter stood, and Aimee followed him to the door. And when he took her in his arms to kiss her good-night, Aimee could taste all of his hunger, all of his passion.

Yet this time she was unable to respond, because she knew in her heart that she could no longer share her body with him without having his love in return.

As though he had sensed a change in her, Peter held her tightly for a moment longer. After giving her another quick, hard kiss, he stepped back. ''I'll call you in the morning.''

And then he was gone.

Aimee closed the door behind him and leaned against it. Funny, she thought as the tears began to slide down her cheeks, how differently this day had turned out from the way she had hoped it would. Instead of celebrating her good fortune and hearing Peter declare his love for her, she was alone and not feeling anything close to happy.

Irritated with herself for her feelings of self-pity, Aimee swiped at the tears. Grabbing a slice of cold pizza, she bit down into a salty anchovy and headed for her studio and her paints.

When Aimee emerged from her studio the next morning, she was tired, but her spirits and sense of optimism were renewed. The early-morning call from Peter apologizing for his surly mood had helped . . . as had the peach roses. After a quick nap, followed by a hot shower, she slipped on her oldest cutoffs and T-shirt.

Time to trade her oil brushes for the thick, coarse ones needed for housepainting, she thought. Arming herself with the new brush her father had sent her and a gallon of canary yellow paint, she headed for the vacant apartment.

By the time two o'clock rolled around, she had finished applying the primer and was halfway through the first coat of paint of the studio apartment. Already the room was beginning to take on a new cheeriness. Still standing atop the ladder, Aimee pulled off the paper ventilation mask that covered her nose and mouth. She wiped a combination of sweat and paint from her forehead with the end of her T-shirt, wincing as the salt from her sweat grazed the knuckles she had scraped on her right hand sanding the walls earlier that week.

"Looks like you could use a break," Liza said. "I just made a pitcher of ice tea. Why don't you come down to the shop and join me for a glass and cool off?"

Arching her back, Aimee looked down at her paint-splattered clothes. She didn't need a mirror to know the rest of her was a mess. "Like this? I'd scare the customers away."

Liza crinkled her nose. "I'm afraid there aren't any to scare away. Sorry," she continued, as though she were afraid that information would distress Aimee. "There hasn't been a soul in the place all morning."

Aimee shrugged, refusing to let the news dampen her spirits. With just a little luck, after the show next month, she would have a dealer to sell her paintings. And if worse came to worst, she could always send a few more over to Sterling's. The money wouldn't be much, but at least it would keep the wolf from the door. "It's still pretty early. Don't worry about it. Things'll pick up."

"You're probably right," Liza said, seeming to relax a bit. "But why don't you come downstairs in the meantime and take a breather?"

"What she could use is her head examined," Peter said from the doorway. He walked over to the window unit and kicked on the air-conditioning. The unit sputtered, and then cool air spilled out into the room. "Dammit, Aimee, this place is like an oven. Don't you know it's dangerous for you to be breathing in those paint fumes without ventilation?"

"Hello, Peter. It's nice to see you, too," Aimee responded with a smile.

"If you didn't want to hire someone to paint this damn place, why didn't you at least ask me to help you?"

Aimee bit back the urge to laugh. "Peter, I know you mean well, but we both know that you're not exactly handy when it comes to repairs around the house."

"I'll say," Liza replied, not bothering to repress her amusement. "Face it, Gallagher, you'd be hard-pressed to do more than change a light bulb."

Peter glared at the blonde. "I would have hired someone to do it for her."

The moment the words were out, Peter knew he had made a mistake.

"Of course. What else?" Liza returned sarcastically.

Ignoring the other woman, he shot a glance toward Aimee, who had gone absolutely still on the ladder. A frown marred her face. This was not turning out at all as he had planned, Peter thought. "Liza, would you please excuse us," he said through gritted teeth. "I'd like to speak with Aimee alone for a moment."

"Would you now? Well, I don't—"

"Liza." Aimee said the name softly, authoritatively.

The two women exchanged looks, and then Liza said, "Well, I need to get back to the shop anyway. Just yell if you need me for anything." After giving Peter a look that said she thought he was the lowest form of plant life, she tipped up her head and walked regally out of the door.

"Before you say a word," Peter said, holding up his hands in surrender, "I'm sorry. I spoke without thinking. I know the very idea of allowing me to do anything that even remotely resembles helping you causes you to have a fit."

"I do not have fits."

Peter sighed. This was definitely not going as he planned. After a sleepless night, he had devised what he thought the perfect scenario by which to convince Aimee to marry him. But at the rate he was going, she would throw him out before he had a chance to ask her. "You're right. I'm sorry... again. How about doing me a favor and coming down off that ladder? It would make talking to you a lot easier."

Once she had done as he requested, Peter suddenly found himself nervous and unsure of how to begin. It had all seemed so simple that morning, when he instructed Doris to purchase an extra ticket for Aimee to accompany him to Chicago. He had had the penthouse suite at the Ritz Carlton reserved for the weekend, and dinner reservations made at the best restaurant in town. He would get his business with Hendrickson out of the way, and then he and Aimee would spend a romantic weekend together. He wanted to make up for the previous evening, and he also wanted to spend some time alone with her—just the two of them.

"Was there something in particular you wanted to talk to me about?" Aimee asked.

This was ridiculous, Peter told himself, feeling foolish over his sudden bout of nerves. "I wanted to invite you to come to Chicago with me for the weekend."

"Which weekend?"

"This weekend. Tomorrow morning."

"Tomorrow?"

"Yes. I've got a meeting scheduled that will take about an hour, but after that we would be free. You had mentioned once that you'd like to see the Chicago Museum of Art..."

"I'm sorry, Peter. I can't go tomorrow."

"And I've made dinner reservations for us at—" Peter stopped, her words finally registering. "You can't go?" he repeated.

"No. I can't. I have a new tenant moving in on Monday. I've got to finish painting this apartment and get it ready before then."

Peter was stunned. He hadn't even considered that she might refuse. "What about Jacques or Liza? Can't you get them to finish for you?"

"I couldn't ask them to do that."

"Why not?" he asked, growing irritated as his plans began to slip away. "They don't seem to have any problem asking you for favors."

Temper flared in her ghost-blue eyes. "I would never take advantage of their friendship that way. The building's my responsibility. Not theirs, and not yours."

He was losing Aimee. He could feel it in his bones, feel it in his gut. The realization only made him more frustrated. And angry. "Obviously your friends and your building are a lot more important to you than I am."

"That's not true."

"No? Then explain to me why you refuse to get rid of this monstrosity."

"Because it's *my* monstrosity," Aimee shot back.

"It's a damn albatross. One that I've offered to take off your hands more than once. At least if you sold or leased the thing to me, I could afford to keep the place in decent shape, which is a lot more than you're able to do."

Her hands positioned on her hips, Aimee came closer to him, standing toe-to-toe with him in a fighter's stance. "This may not be a showplace, but it is my home and I love it." She lifted her chin a notch. "For your information, I'm doing just fine, and I'm going to do even better. I've sold a few of my paintings recently, and I'll be in Kay Sloane's exhibit next month. It's just a matter of time before my art starts paying off, and then I can afford to hire someone to keep the place in good shape."

"I've already offered to hire repairmen for you. Hell, I've asked you to marry me," Peter reminded her. "If you would use a little common sense, you'd take me up on both offers. At least as my wife you wouldn't have to kill yourself trying to keep up this place. I'd hire someone to do it for you. And you certainly wouldn't have to sweat participating in some amateur exhibit."

"Thanks, but no thanks. My building and my art are doing just fine without your help."

"Really?" Peter continued, too caught up in his own emotional struggle over his feelings for Aimee to recognize the extent of her anger and pride. He ran an appraising glance over the partially painted room, the cracked windowpanes and chipped molding, before turning his probing gaze back to her. "From where I'm standing, it doesn't look to me like you're doing too good of a job at either."

Peter's words struck her like a blow, making her exceedingly conscious of her threadbare shorts and paint-splattered shirt. Still, she refused to be intimidated. "Like I said, I'm doing just fine."

"You call selling your paintings in a dump like Sterling's for peanuts, just to get enough money to pay the repair bills on this place, doing fine?"

Shock raced through Aimee. "How did you know I sold my paintings through Sterling's?"

"How do you think I know? I know because I'm the one who bought them!"

Fury, white and hot, ripped through Aimee. What a fool she had been! Aimee told herself. How had she kidded herself into believing some collector had actually stumbled upon her work and liked it? "Why?" she demanded, as all the old insecurities about her talent returned to plague her.

"Because it's the only way I could help you."

"Are you sure, Peter? You're sure it's not because you didn't believe anyone else would think my work was good enough?" Her voice broke. "Or maybe it was because *you* don't believe I'm good enough."

"Aimee, that's not true." He started to touch her, but she backed away from him. Peter's hand fell to his side. "I was only trying to help. I knew you needed the money."

"What I needed was for you to love me, to trust me. I can see now that that was too much to ask."

"Aimee, don't." He reached out to her, speared his fingers through her cropped hair. "I've never wanted another woman more than I want you. I still want you," he said before covering her mouth with his own.

Her heart feeling as though it were breaking, Aimee remained lifeless in his arms. When he finally lifted his head and looked at her with tortured eyes, pleading eyes, Aimee hardened her heart. For her own sake, she had to end it now. "I know you want me, Peter. But wanting is not enough anymore. At least not for me." How did she explain to him that she needed to fuel more than his desire for her? She needed his love. "I need more, Peter. More than you can give."

"What are you saying?"

"I'm saying the affair's over. We always said it would last as long as it was what we both wanted. Well, it's not what I want any more."

Peter searched her face for long moments, then released her. "So much for your being in love with me, huh? I guess I was right after all. A marriage between us wouldn't have lasted. Hell, we couldn't even make it through an affair."

Aimee dismissed the bitterness in his voice. "No, we didn't, did we? Maybe if I hadn't fallen in love with you, we could have at least made it through the affair. But we can't change who we are or what we feel. And the truth is that while you may lust for me, you don't love me. I want...I deserve...someone who can give me both." She needed the emotional bonds that went with their lovemaking—the emotional commitment that Peter was unable to make.

His expression softened. "You're right. You deserve the very best, Aimee. I only wish that I had been the one to give it to you."

"So do I," Aimee whispered as he walked out the door and out of her life.

Ten

Peter came awake with a start. Sitting up, he kicked away
the tangled sheets and thrust his hands through his hair. His
fingers came away damp with perspiration.

His breathing still ragged, he took slow, measured breaths
and waited for the last remnants of the nightmare to leave
him. The confounded dream was becoming more frequent,
too frequent, he thought. He didn't need a shrink to tell him
that the ending of his affair with Aimee was the reason he
had had the nightmare again. Hell, he had had the stupid
dream any number of times since she had kicked him out of
her life, nearly a month ago.

And he had managed to survive the worst of those first
few weeks without her. Of course, he admitted, the extensive travel schedule he had set for himself was the major
reason. It seemed only fitting, since he had put off travel-
ing in order to remain in New Orleans with Aimee, that it
was because of her that he felt the need to get away.

Spending so much of his time with Aimee had caused him
to neglect the part of his business that he had always found

most interesting—acquiring and discovering new art. Unfortunately, resuming the quest had not proved nearly as
fulfilling as it had once been. In fact, it had made him wonder how he had ever managed to spend so many of his wak-
ing hours in such relentless pursuit—especially since beating
out other collectors at auctions or trying to scoop a valuable piece before it was put on the market held only mini-
mal satisfaction now. Even signing the maddening
Hendrickson, an artist whose work he was sure would one
day command a fortune, had proven anticlimactic.

Face it, Gallagher, he told himself as he yawned. *There is
no longer any thrill in the chase.* But the back-to-back trips
had served their purpose, he conceded. At least not being in
the same city with Aimee had kept him from attempting to
see her. Unfortunately, it had not kept him from thinking of
her.

And he had been thinking of Aimee. In truth, she had
seldom been out of his thoughts. He had thought of her
when he wandered through the museum in Chicago, and
when he dined alone at the hotel. He had thought of her
when he jetted to Paris and visited the Louvre without her.
He had missed her. Not just making love with her, but talking to her and hearing the sound of her laughter, as well. He
had missed being with her, sharing bits and pieces of his day,
bits and pieces of his life, with her. He had even missed listening to her talk about the disasters at the building and her
wacky tenants. He had missed her far more than he had ever
thought possible.

But it was returning to New Orleans that morning and
discovering the invitation to Aimee's exhibit that had
brought on the latest bout of sleeplessness...and with it the
infernal nightmare.

Swinging his legs over the edge of the bed, Peter planted
his feet on the floor. He shoved his fingers through his hair.
He had taken enough psychology courses in college to recognize that his being locked in the vault and abandoned was
synonymous with his being locked out of Aimee's life.

Not that he blamed her. He didn't. He didn't even resent the fact that the end of their affair had also ended any chance he might have of reclaiming the building. Strange how getting the place back didn't seem to matter as much to him as it once had. At best, it had been a foolish quest on his part, Peter realized. He was no longer even sure what he had expected to gain by getting Aimee to sell him the place—except perhaps redemption from his father, for finally fulfilling his promise to the old man. How he had expected to gain that redemption from his father's grave, he didn't know.

No. What he resented was the fact that he had managed to hurt Aimee in the process. He had never meant to hurt her. She certainly hadn't deserved to be hurt. But he had hurt her all the same. And it was because he didn't want to hurt her further that he had accepted her decision to end things between them and forced himself to stay away.

Peter looked at the clock on his nightstand, which read 8:30. After picking up his mail and messages from the gallery, he had evidently collapsed on the bed and slept for nearly ten hours.

He stretched his arms over his head and attempted to work out the kinks in his shoulders and neck before glancing out the window of his condo. Except for the sprinkling of a few stars that had managed to break through the shroud of clouds, darkness filled the skyline. Even the sliver of moon had been swallowed in the heavy cloud cover.

Passing his hand over his face, he wiped away the last remnants of sleep. Looking at the clock again, he caught sight of the invitation to Aimee's exhibit. He picked up the bright-colored parchment from the nightstand, where he had propped it up earlier. He ran his fingertip across the letters of her name and reread the announcement inviting him to the exhibit that evening.

Did Aimee know he had been sent an invitation? He was a major dealer, and it would have been foolish to leave his name off the guest list. Chances were she didn't even know he had been invited.

Or maybe, just maybe, she had invited him herself. Was it possible that she had missed him just as much as he had missed her? His pulse picked up speed at the notion. At the same time, he told himself it was far more likely that she didn't care one way or another whether he came. In fact, she probably wouldn't want him to come.

The idea that she might not want him there rankled him, even as he admitted she had every right to feel that way. Aimee had been right to kick him out of her life, Peter told himself as he headed for the bathroom. He turned on the water and stepped under the punishing-hot spray.

Aimee deserved better than him. She deserved a man who loved her—not a man who wasn't even capable of the emotion. That he was incapable of the sentiment, he had no doubt. It was probably one of the few things that he and Leslie had agreed upon. That, and his ex-wife's desire for him to make her a star.

Strange, but it was on these very same things that he and Aimee had never agreed.

As the water pummeled his skin and washed away the weariness of the transatlantic flight, he reminded himself of all the reasons he should stay away from Aimee.

But even as he told himself that he shouldn't go to the exhibit, that he would be an unwelcome guest, he knew he was going to go. If for no other reason than to simply see her again and discover for himself just how much she now hated him.

Twenty minutes later, when he entered the hotel and was directed to the ballroom where the exhibit was being held, Peter told himself he was a fool for coming. If he hadn't already garnered Aimee's hatred with his attempt to help her by purchasing her paintings, he would surely earn it now by showing up tonight. This was the night of her first professional triumph. He was the last person with whom she would want to share it. Besides, she would never believe that he truly wished her well, or that he did believe she was a talented artist.

"Can I see your invitation, sir?" the usher at the door asked.

Peter retrieved the card from the pocket of his tuxedo jacket and handed it to the young man. As he entered the room, he scanned the crowd. He was impressed by the number of collectors and dealers, not to mention moneyed patrons, that Kay Sloane had managed to deliver. Several of his own clients were in attendance. Moving along the edge of the room, he searched for a glimpse of Aimee.

"Peter, I didn't know you would be here tonight," Mrs. Armstrong, one of his wealthiest clients, said upon spotting him. "When I stopped in at Gallagher's last week, I was told you were out of town."

"I was. I just returned this morning."

The older woman smiled at him, deepening the laugh lines around her eyes. "Well, I'm glad you're back. I could use your opinion on a painting I'm thinking of purchasing. It's a most interesting abstract by one of these new artists. Would you mind taking a look at it and telling me what you think of it as an investment?"

Peter hesitated, wondering if the painting in question was one of Aimee's. Until now, he hadn't given it much thought, but he suddenly realized that a word from him could make or break the career of the artist in question. For the first time, Peter experienced a measure of irritation at having such power. "Do you like it, Phoebe?" he finally asked.

Diamonds winked from the lobes of her ears as she tilted her head and looked up at him questioningly. "Why, yes, I do."

"Then you don't need me to look at it for you. You have an excellent eye for art. If you like it, buy it."

"Really?" the woman asked.

"Really," he said, before excusing himself to go in search of Aimee.

Surprised by what he had just done, Peter smiled at the radical change in his own behavior. Eight months ago, the businessman in him would never have done such a thing. He would have worked the room, checked out the exhibits and determined the buyers' levels of interest. After doing so, he would have signed the most promising artists before the party was over. And then he would have encouraged the Phoebe Armstrongs to purchase the paintings through him.

But that had been before Aimee came into his life. Before she taught him to look at a painting and appreciate it with his heart and not with a calculator in his hand.

It had been before she shared her laughter and her love of life with him. It had been before she walked out of his life and took all the laughter in it, and the only real love he had ever known, along with her.

"Champagne?" a waitress asked, holding a tray of crystal flutes filled with the golden liquid.

"No thanks." Peter moved toward the center of the room, searching for a glimpse of familiar dark hair framing a pair of haunting blue eyes. He was beginning to wonder if he had arrived too late when he spotted her standing next to an abstract—an explosion of bright red and silver and blue on canvas.

She wore a dress of some sheer white lacy fabric that gently skimmed her body and fell loosely about her thighs. Jagged strips of silver that resembled small lightning bolts dangled from her ears and flashed through the strands of short hair scattered about her ears. In this sea of designer cocktail dresses and tuxedos, Aimee's simple attire stood out like a precious stone among fakes. She smiled and her ghost-blue eyes gleamed like rare gems as Liza hugged her, then kissed her cheek, evidently offering congratulations. Peter frowned as Jacques came forward and kissed both of Aimee's cheeks. And when he lifted her up and hugged her Peter caught sight of the Sold tag on the painting.

She'd done it, Peter thought, just as she had always wanted to do...just as he had wanted and at the same time feared she would do. Realization struck him with the force of a body blow. All these months, he had kidded himself. He had told himself it was Aimee's building that he wanted when all he really wanted was Aimee herself.

As he watched Aimee bask in the praise of her friends, Peter realized that what he had feared was not her success, but her leaving him once she had become successful.

She was on her way to becoming a star—a star with no room in her life for him. He had lost her, Peter admitted, feeling as though something inside him had died. Deep down, he had always known she could be a part of his life only temporarily. Perhaps that was why he had refused to admit even to himself the extent of her talent. Perhaps that was why he had been unable to tell her that he hadn't bought her paintings from Sterling's to help her, but because the businessman in him knew they would be worth a great deal more someday. But primarily he had bought them because he wanted to hold on to her. In the end, he had lost her anyway.

Coming tonight had been a mistake, Peter decided, unable to banish the inexplicable ache in his chest. He had to get out of here. Now. Before he made a fool of himself and begged her to give him another chance.

He had never begged anyone for anything in his life. Not his parents. Not Leslie. He wasn't about to start now. He watched as Aimee shook hands with Kay Sloane and a man and woman. She positively glowed.

He had to forget about her, Peter told himself. Confused, the ache in his chest growing more painful by the second, he started to turn away.

He isn't going to come, Aimee told herself as she forced her gaze away from the doorway and shook hands with the couple who had purchased one of her paintings. Her jaws ached from all the smiling she had had to do this evening. This should be the happiest night of her life, and yet all she wanted to do was go home, crawl into her bed and cry.

And it was all Peter Gallagher's fault.

"Donald and I simply fell in love with the colors," the new owner of her painting said.

"Thank you," Aimee murmured politely as she shifted her gaze back to the doorway. Something, perhaps the sense that she was being watched from afar, made her cut a glance toward her left.

"And the composition..."

Her heart seemed to lurch in her chest. It was Peter. "I'm sorry. Would you please excuse me?" Not waiting for an answer, Aimee hurried toward him. "Peter! Peter, wait!"

Peter spun around at the sound of her voice. His deep blue eyes lit up momentarily. Was it joy she had glimpsed in their depths? If only she was better at reading him, Aimee told herself. If only he wasn't so good at hiding what he was feeling.

When she finally reached him, it took everything in her not to throw herself into his arms. She searched his face for some inkling of what he was feeling. "Did you just get here?"

"A few minutes ago. I was just about to leave."

The words were like a slap. "You were going to leave without even speaking to me? Without at least wishing me good luck?"

"Doesn't look like you need any luck." He took her hands in his and brought them to his lips. He kissed her fingers. Still holding her hands, he whispered, "Congratulations, Aimee."

"Thanks," she said, her heart beating wildly. "I hoped you would come tonight, Peter. I told myself if you did, it would be a sign."

"*You* sent me the invitation?" Peter asked, his surprise evident.

"Yes."

"I'm glad that you did. But why? I wasn't sure you would ever want to see me again."

"Because this is the most important night of my career. Success or failure, I wanted to share it with you." In truth she had been searching for sight of him all evening, and until she saw him, the success she had prayed for for so long had held little joy for her—without Peter to share it.

Something deep and powerful flickered in his eyes. He squeezed her fingers. "Aimee, I—"

"There you are," Jacques said, coming to her side with Liza in tow. "Gallagher." He acknowledged and dismissed Peter with a nod of his head.

"Gaston."

"There is a gentleman with a gallery in New York who wishes to speak to you," Jacques told her.

"I wouldn't be surprised if he offers Aimee a contract," Liza added.

Aimee flushed at her friends' blatant attempts to rub Peter's nose in her success.

But if it bothered him, he didn't show it. He merely smiled and looking at her, he said, "If I had been a good business-man, I would have signed Aimee up for Gallagher's myself a long time ago."

Liza gave him a saccharine smile. "Judging by the way things have gone tonight, I'd say you were certainly a fool to let her get away."

Aimee sucked in her breath.

"And I'd have to agree with you. Losing Aimee was one of the worst mistakes of my life," Peter said quietly.

"Come on, Aimee. You really do need to get back." Liza tugged gently on her arm. When she didn't respond, Liza gave her another tug. "Aimee?"

"I think our Aimee is where she wishes to be," Jacques said. He took hold of Liza's fingers, forcing her to release her hold on Aimee.

"But what about the gallery owner from New York?" Liza protested.

"I'll suggest he meet with Aimee another time. Come along, Liza, you can bat your pretty green eyes at him on Aimee's behalf."

Liza scowled at Jacques. "I do not bat my eyes at men."

"Of course you do. You're a shameful flirt when it suits your purposes. It's something I've been meaning to discuss with you."

"I have nothing to say to you."

"Ah, but there is much I wish to say to you, *ma chére*," Jacques replied as he led Liza away.

"I don't know what's gotten into the two of them,"
Aimee said. "They've been acting strange lately. I'm sorry
for the way they treated you, Peter. I guess they're sort of
protective of me. It's been a rough few weeks."

"For me, too."

Aimee swallowed, pleased by his admission. "Thanks for
coming tonight."

"I tried to stay away, but I couldn't. I've had Doris book
me out of town to meet new artists, go to auctions, other
exhibits. Anything to keep me out of New Orleans...to keep
me away from you. But as soon as I came back...as soon
as I saw the invitation, I knew I had to come. I had to see
you. I couldn't stay away any longer."

"I'm glad you didn't."

He squeezed her fingers and pulled her closer. "I know
I'm being selfish. You've probably made plans to go out
with your friends to celebrate. But I have to ask anyway.
Will you—" He hesitated, as though searching for the right
words. "Will you at least let me see you home?"

Aimee looked up at Peter, and her heart seemed to stop.
She had never seen him look quite so sad, so unsure of
himself. His vulnerability and unhappiness tore at her. She
had never been very good at telling Peter no. She wasn't any
better now. "It wasn't anything carved in stone. I'm sure
Jacques and Liza will understand." At least she hoped they
would. She scanned the room for her friends, and when she
didn't see either of them, Aimee took it as another sign and
just as she had done all of her life, she listened to her heart.
"The exhibit will be wrapping up in another ten minutes.
Maybe they decided to go on without me."

"You're sure?" he asked.

"I'm sure."

And then they were racing for the exit, ignoring the surprised expressions on people's faces as they hurried down
the escalator steps, too impatient to wait for it to descend.
Laughing, their hands clasped together, they rushed out of
the hotel and into the night.

Thunder boomed in the distance as they turned down the street and started toward the French Quarter. Lightning flashed overhead, illuminating a street sign. Rain fell in huge drops from the sky, splattering on pavement still warm from the sun's heat, sending up tiny swirls of steam like wisps of smoke.

Aimee threw back her head and laughed. And Peter laughed along with her. It didn't matter that her hair was plastered to her head, that the new white dress that she had thought so pretty and had bought especially for tonight's exhibit would probably be ruined. It didn't even matter that the antique silver shoes with delicate ribbon straps that she had discovered in the trunk of things left to her by Aunt Tessie would be hopelessly stained from the rain splashing on her feet and ankles. She continued to run down the street, clinging to Peter's hand and he clinging just as tightly to hers.

By the time they reached her building, Aimee was completely out of breath and wet from head to toe.

"Where's your key?" Peter asked, his own breathing a bit ragged.

"It's open."

Shoving open the door, Peter ushered her inside the hallway of the building and closed the door behind them. The small, dark alcove, filled with the sound of their breathing, added to the air of intimacy that had begun with their race from the hotel. "You're soaked to the skin," he whispered as he allowed his eyes to adjust to the dim lighting.

"So are you," Aimee informed him. She laughed, the sound a haunting melody that he had heard countless times in his dreams this past month. Peter shut his eyes, realizing once more how very much he had missed her.

She pulled at his tie, and he opened his eyes in time to see it fall at his feet, a lump of wet black fabric. "I think you're going to need a new tie and cummerbund. Maybe even a new tux."

"I don't care."

Laughing, she leaned against the banister. A trace of a smile still curved her lips as she glanced up the steep, winding staircase. "You know, when I make that first million, I really am going to install an elevator in this place."

The smile on his own lips faded as Aimee started up the steps. The wispy dress she wore clung to her bare legs, silhouetting each line, each curve, of her body. She turned to him. In the faint light of the stairwell, and with the flimsy material plastered to her skin, he could see the lean curve of her hips, the edge of her panties. His breath caught in his throat as his gaze traveled upward, to where the dark nipples of her breasts pebbled against the sheer fabric.

"Peter?"

He heard her call his name, heard the rain beating against the wooden door, the wind whistling through the cracks and crevices as the storm played out its frenzied tune.

But the storm outside was no match for the storm of emotions raging through him. At that moment, all the hunger, all the loneliness, of the past few weeks without Aimee came to him in a rush.

"Peter, is something wrong?"

He held out his hand, and when Aimee took it, he pulled her into his arms. He held her tightly, breathing in the clean scent of rain on her skin, the faint trace of roses that always seemed to be a part of her.

When she eased back and eyed him curiously, Peter captured a raindrop that was clinging to her cheek with his fingertip. He brought it to his lips. Then, unable to resist, he lowered his head and kissed her. In defiance of the storm raging outside and the one raging inside him, he kissed her gently, tenderly.

When Aimee slid her arms up to circle his neck and pressed her body next to him, Peter felt as if he had come home at last. "Ah, Aimee," he said, his voice unsteady "I've missed you so much. So very much."

Her ghost-blue eyes filled with emotion. "I've missed you, too," she whispered. Taking his face in her hands, she deepened the kiss.

After weeks of being without her, he felt like a man who had been lost in a storm and had stumbled upon a safe haven. He cupped one of her breasts. The nipple seemed to spring to life at his touch, fueling his thirst for more.

Peter could feel himself growing harder by the second, his shaft straining against his slacks as his need for her became even more painful.

Aimee pulled him to her and opened her mouth to him. Peter bit back a groan. When she pressed her femininity against his hardness, Peter realized her need was as great as his own. And he realized that what he desired more than anything this moment was to satisfy her need, to give her pleasure. He slipped his hand between them.

Aimee moaned in protest as Peter withdrew slightly and eased his hand along the curve of her hip, down her stomach, to the warm, pulsating juncture between her thighs. His mouth left hers and moved to the rain-drenched skin of her throat before closing over the wet fabric that covered her nipple. She sucked in her breath. She was still reeling from the shock of feeling the warmth and moistness of Peter's mouth through the sheer clothing when he lifted the skirt of her dress and peeled it away from her skin. His fingers continued their quest along her leg to the inside of her thigh.

The sensations rushing through her body were delicious, but they weren't enough. She couldn't continue to love him, to make love with him and not have his love in return. "No, Peter," she said, pulling herself free. She couldn't return to the vicious cycle she had been in before. "I can't. I don't want this."

Peter froze. Panic seized him at her words. She had to want him. He needed Aimee to want him. He looked at her mouth, swollen from his kisses, at her eyes, still warm with desire. "You're lying, Aimee. You want me. Just as much as I want you. It's the one thing we've always agreed on." He pulled her back into his arms. "I want you," he said, his voice hoarse with desire. Taking her hand, he pressed it to him. "Feel, Aimee. Feel how much I want you...how much I need you...only you."

"It's not enough, Peter. Wanting's not enough for me."

Her words sent fear clawing down his spine. He couldn't lose her, not now, when he had just realized how much she meant to him. "You once said you loved me. This ... what I feel for you is as close as I can come to love. It's all that I have to give," he said, his voice cracking. "I want you, Aimee. And, heaven help me, I know I'm being unfair. But I need for you to want me."

At her silence, Peter pinned her with his gaze. "Tell me I haven't destroyed what you once felt for me. Say it, Aimee. I need to hear you say it. Tell me you still love me."

Her emotions were already in turmoil, and the plea in Peter's voice was her undoing. "I love you. I've always loved you."

He crushed her to him. And this time when he kissed her she could taste the hunger and the need. He loved her, Aimee realized. He didn't know it, but Peter was in love with her. The realization sent a burst of joy surging through her, fueling her own desire.

And this time when Peter slid his hand up her bare leg and inside her panties, Aimee didn't even think of protesting. She clung to his shoulders, her body hungering for and anticipating his touch. As he stroked the sensitive nub of her femininity, Aimee gasped. "Peter," she cried out as the first wave of pleasure flowed over her.

"Promise me you won't ever say no to me again, Aimee. Not about this. Never about this," he murmured.

"I promise," she whispered as he renewed the gentle stroking that sent her climbing toward the peak again. And just as the first shudder gripped her, Peter took her mouth and swallowed her cries of pleasure while she rode out the rest of the storm.

Eleven

Peter held Aimee in his arms for long moments as the last tremors of the climax ran through her. His own body throbbed with his need for her. He still desired Aimee desperately. Yet he had found great satisfaction in giving her his pleasure.

"*Ma chère,* if you will let go of me for a moment, I will get my key." At the sound of Jacques's voice, followed by a feminine murmur, Peter scooped Aimee up in his arms and started up the stairway.

"Peter, you can't carry me up these stairs. They're too steep."

He silenced her with a kiss. Keeping one eye open, he managed to make it to the top of the stairs. He stopped in front of the door of her apartment. "Did you bother to lock this one?"

Smiling, she shook her head.

"For once, I'm glad you didn't."

"So am I."

She began unbuttoning his shirt. The onyx studs hit the floor with a thud, and Peter kicked the door closed. Struggling against the fierce urge to lay her on the floor and bury himself in her sweet warmth, he whispered, "I want you. More than I've ever wanted anyone or anything. But if it's still not enough . . . if you want me to go . . . I will."

She touched his face. "Peter, I—"

"Wait. Let me finish. But if I stay, Aimee, it's for keeps. I want more than an affair this time. I want you to marry me. I know there are a lot of things we need to work out, but I'm willing to try, if you are." He searched her face for a reaction to his ultimatum. For once, her expressive face gave no hint of what she was thinking. Bracing himself, Peter asked, "What's it going to be? Do I stay or do I leave?"

In answer, Aimee curled her arms around his neck and drew his head down to hers.

Foolish, stubborn, sweet Peter, she thought. Parting her lips, she offered him all that she had, all that she was, and took all that he gave in return. He *was* in love with her and he didn't even know it.

Oh, he hadn't given her the words, Aimee admitted, smiling, as he carried her into the bedroom. Perhaps he never would. But he had declared his love for her, just as surely as if he had shouted it from the rooftop.

His strong, sure fingers trembled as he unfastened the silver-and-pearl buttons of her dress. The garment fell in a puddle of white around her feet. "Ah, Aimee. You're so beautiful," he said, circling the tips of her breasts with his fingers.

The smile on her lips faded as he repeated the motion with his tongue. He planted a row of kisses down her midriff, along her waist, on her quivering stomach. He stripped away her panties, and his fingers sought out the dark curls between her legs. And when he eased opened her thighs, parted the feminine flesh and stroked her with his tongue, Aimee gasped. Curling her fingers into his shoulders, she hung on to him, afraid that her legs would fail her.

Lightning flashed outside the bedroom window, and her heart thundered in echo. And when the first wave of pleasure shook her, Aimee wasn't sure whether the crash that followed was from the fiery storm going on outside or from the one going on in her bedroom. Peter continued to taunt, to taste, to suckle, the tiny nub of her desire, until Aimee thought she would go mad. Each time he brought her to the brink, taking her higher and higher, to that precipice between pleasure and ecstasy. And when she thought she could stand it no longer, he carried her over the edge into the heat of the storm.

Aimee clung to him, her body shivering as another wave of pleasure took her. "Please, no more," she pleaded, feeling as though she would shatter. Cupping his head, she drew him to his feet. "Make love to me, Peter. Let me make love to you."

Rain pelted against the windows, loud slaps demanding entry. Peter ripped off his jacket and shirt in one movement. The rest of his clothes followed.

When he joined her on the bed, Aimee closed her fingers around his shaft. "Sweet heaven," Peter muttered, sucking in his breath. He closed his eyes.

Aimee felt the shudder run through his body and delighted in the knowledge that she could affect him so strongly. As he eased his leg between her thighs, she guided him to her.

His face was so close, his mouth so near, Aimee wasn't sure where his breath ended and hers began. She wasn't sure if it was his heart she heard hammering, or her own.

When he thrust into her, Aimee caught her breath. He waited, giving her body a moment to adjust. Then, slowly, he began moving inside her, filling her, then withdrawing almost completely, only to enter her again, repeating the pattern of sensual torment and pleasure he had performed with his tongue.

"I can't give you the hearts-and-flowers fairy tale you wanted, Aimee. But I swear, I'll give you everything that's in me, everything I can."

"Then give me everything," she told him, arching her body to meet him.

His eyes flashed, a heated silver that matched the lightning illuminating the night sky outside her window. The storm outside raged on, unleashing a fury that seem to echo Peter's quickening thrusts. The storm outside exploded, and Peter lifted her hips and drove into her a final time. And as the thunder rumbled and crashed, Peter cried out her name, and Aimee followed him into the storm.

Peter opened his eyes to the sun filtering through the window and warming his cheek. He stretched. It had been the first decent night's sleep that he had had in months. Not that he had slept very much, he thought, smiling. He and Aimee had made love long and often into the night. And each time, she had been more wonderful, more giving, than the time before. And between their rounds of lovemaking, he had slept. Peacefully. With no cursed nightmares.

Stretching out his arm, he patted the empty space where Aimee should be. There was a sense of rightness, of completeness, in awaking in Aimee's bed. He had felt this same way last night, each time she whispered her love to him. Perhaps he was unable to give her the love she wanted. But he would keep his promise to her. He would give her all that he had to give.

His stomach grumbled. Flipping away the sheet from his naked body, Peter abandoned the bed and went in search of Aimee and food.

The sound of the shower running and an off-key show tune coming from the bathroom led him to her. For long seconds, he contemplated joining her, but when his stomach grumbled again, he headed for the kitchen instead.

After grabbing a cup of coffee, he started back toward the bedroom, but then he spotted the door to Aimee's studio. It was open. Peter stood in the doorway and waited for the old familiar feelings of failure to strike him. It was in this room, the room he had promised his father as a studio, that his sense of failure had always been most prevalent. Perhaps because it was this room that most represented his father's dreams, and his own failure to see them to fruition.

The feelings never came.

Stepping inside the studio, Peter scanned the room and realized it held the same feeling of rightness that the rest of the apartment did. It was Aimee's apartment now, just as this studio was now hers. And any feelings of failure he had once experienced here were gone, just as was his foolish desire to reclaim the building.

More relaxed, Peter prowled about the studio, suddenly curious to discover the work that she loved so passionately. He studied the paintings. She really was good, he thought, impressed by the sheer force of life that she had managed to imbue her work with. Sipping his coffee, he moved from one painting to the next. The art connoisseur and businessman in him grew excited by what he saw.

As he turned, he caught sight of a piece she had positioned in the center of the room. A drape covered the piece, but had slipped off of one end. From what he could see, it was a portrait, which surprised him. Although he knew she had done a couple of portraits in the past, most of the works in her studio were abstracts. Growing more curious, Peter set down his cup and moved over to the painting. He pulled the drape away.

His own face stared back at him. Peter swallowed. Stunned, he continued to stare at the portrait. It wasn't the first portrait that had been done of him. He had been painted before—his father had done one of him as a child, and Leslie had given him one shortly after their wedding. But this one was different. The eyes of the man in this portrait had a warmth, a vulnerability, that he didn't possess. His own eyes were cold, hard. Robotlike, Leslie had called them.

"Does that frown mean you don't like it?" Aimee asked.

Peter looked up. She stood in the doorway, a thick pink towel wrapped around her body. Beads of water clung to the ends of her short dark hair. Several drops fell and slid lazily down her neck. Her face was free of makeup, and her ghost-blue eyes were wide and uncertain. To him, no woman had ever looked more beautiful.

He loved her, Peter realized. All these months he had been telling himself it was the building, it was lust, it was sex. And all the while, he had been in love with her.

Aimee bit her bottom lip. Her face was a study of uncertainty. "For heaven's sake, Peter, say *something*. I know portraits aren't the norm for me. I mean, I've only done a few. And to tell you the truth, I like the freedom of expression in abstracts." She pulled the towel more snugly about her. "But since my lessons with Jacques have been going so well, I thought I'd give it a try. I mean, I always thought you'd make a great subject. And I—" She let out a breath. "Well, if you don't like it, just say so."

"It's wonderful, Aimee."

Her eyes lit up, and she moved over to stand beside him. "Do you really think so?"

"Yes." Peter slid his arm around her. "Do you really see me this way?"

"What way?"

"I have no delusions about myself, Aimee. I know what most people think of me, what they say. I'm not an easy man, and I've never been accused of being gentle. Yet here…" He motioned to the painting. "You make me look almost kind."

Taking his face in her hands, Aimee whispered, "You are kind, Peter Gallagher. You're probably one of the kindest men I know."

"If there's any kindness in me, it's because of you. I love you, Aimee."

Aimee's heart stopped, then started again.

"It's true. I only realized it myself a little while ago."

Unable to speak, Aimee threw her arms around his neck and kissed him. How long had she waited, prayed, to hear him say those words? "I love you," she whispered, but when she would have kissed him again, he pulled back.

"And I love you. But there's something I have to tell you. A confession, really. It's about this building…"

A short time later, when he had told her about once own-ing the building, and his quest to reclaim it, Aimee's heart was beating wildly, making her afraid to ask the question that had been nagging at her since he began his story. But she had to know. "Getting the building—is it the reason you asked me to marry you?"

"At first, the building was the reason I told myself I be-came involved with you. I wanted it, but certainly never had any intention of asking you to marry me just to get it. I'd sworn that I'd never marry anyone again. But then I found myself asking you to marry me anyway.

"Once I proposed and you accepted, I told myself that if we married, I'd pay you fairly for the building and then convert it for Gallagher's. But then you threw my ring and the prenuptial agreement back in my face. It wasn't long afterward that I realized it wasn't the building I wanted, but you. Only your being an artist kept getting in the way, con-fusing me."

"Why?"

"It's crazy, because I was, in a sense, willing to use you, but I was worried you'd end up using me, instead, to fur-ther your career. That's why I refused to even consider your work."

"That's what I thought you were thinking," she told him.

"But then Edmond showed up, and then I realized I'd really screwed up big-time. I didn't admit it for a long time, but what I was really afraid of was that you would become a success and I would lose you."

"The way you lost Leslie?"

"Losing Leslie hurt my pride and my bank balance, not me. What I felt for her wasn't love. Not even close."

"She broke your heart," Aimee reminded him.

"She wounded my pride and forced me to break a prom-ise I'd made to my father. You on the other hand," he said, gathering her into his arms, "you *can* break my heart." A shadow crossed his face, and he pulled her even closer, holding her so tight Aimee thought she would break. "Tell me you love me," he demanded, as though he were afraid she would disappear.

Confused, Aimee didn't understand the source of the demons that drove Peter. She only knew she wanted desperately to drive them away. "I love you, Peter," she whispered. "I'll always love you."

"Show me," he said, his voice a husky plea.

Seconds later, when he had stripped away her towel and guided her onto his hard shaft, Aimee lifted her face to the sun streaming through the windows. And as she gave him her love and her body, she told herself that somehow, some way, she would find a way to banish Peter's demons and teach him to trust once again.

"I hate like hell the idea of leaving you for so long," Peter told Aimee several hours later.

"Me, too."

He bit into the peanut-butter-and-jelly sandwich, the only food he had deemed edible in her apartment. It had been nearly thirty-six hours since he had forced himself to eat the chicken salad Doris had left in his refrigerator with a note instructing him to eat. Food had been the last thing on his mind once he and Aimee returned from the exhibit. After sleeping most of the morning away and spending the rest of it making love with Aimee, he had given little thought to his stomach.

Until now.

Peter smiled. Now, even peanut butter and jelly on whole-wheat bread tasted delicious, although he had forgone the addition of the sliced bananas that Aimee had offered. Lord, but he was going to miss her. "Are you sure you can't come with me? I could extend the trip another week or two, and we could take a real honeymoon. You'll love Paris, Aimee. There's so much to see, the museums—"

"Stop! You're not playing fair," she complained, holding up her hand in protest.

"I know," he admitted. But it didn't make his wish for her to accompany him any less.

"As much as I'd like to go with you, it really would be a mistake for me not to capitalize on last night's success. Not to mention how unfair it would be to Kay. I'm supposed to be meeting with her tomorrow afternoon. She's trying to get the state to fund more art programs, and she's hoping to use the success of last night's exhibit as an example. I owe it to her to follow through on the publicity she's lined up. I hope you understand."

"I do." Leaning across the table, he wiped a smudge of grape jelly from the corner of her mouth with his fingertip, then brushed her lips with his own. "But I still had to ask."

"And I'm glad you did." Aimee smiled. Her eyes sparkled like pale blue diamonds as she took another sip of milk. "How long will you be gone?"

"Almost a month," Peter said, dreading the idea of being away from Aimee for that length of time. Now that he had finally realized he was in love with her, he wondered how he had ever managed to get through the past few weeks without her. One thing was sure, once they were husband and wife, there would be no more long separations and no more nights when the two of them did not share the same bed. "I could kick myself for telling Doris to schedule all those appointments. If it wasn't so late, and I wasn't sure I'd offend some of my best contacts by not showing up, I'd cancel the entire trip and reschedule it later, when you can come with me."

"If it makes you feel any better, I probably won't be having much free time, anyway. Kay told me last night that she had had a couple of requests from the local media for interviews, and she suggested the artists involved participate. Between that, Jacques's second show next week, the shop, and the new painting I'm working on, I suspect I'm going to be pretty busy myself."

"Not too busy to plan a wedding, I hope."

"Oh, I think I can squeeze it in," she said, grinning.

"You'd better squeeze it in," Peter said in a mock-threatening voice. Standing, he moved to Aimee's side and pulled her to her feet. "But in case you forget, I plan to call and remind you."

Laughing, Aimee wound her arms around his neck. "I love you, Peter Gallagher."

"And I love you, Aimee Lawrence. I don't intend to wait a minute longer than I have to before I make you my wife." The thought of Aimee as his wife sent a thrill of anticipation down his spine. She hadn't mentioned the prenuptial agreement again, and neither had he. Even though he knew it was only fair to tell her she would still have to agree to sign it, he couldn't bring himself to do it now. Not when he would be too far away to make her see reason and the need for the document.

Cupping her bottom with his hands, he fit her against him. His body responded instantly. "If you didn't have your heart set on a church wedding with your family, I'd insist we take off for the coast right now and get married by a justice of the peace. Then I'd stop at the first hotel we came to and get started on our honeymoon."

Aimee wiggled her bottom slightly, and Peter bit back a groan as he felt his shaft grow even harder. He already felt guilty over the number of times he had made love to her during the night and this morning. He had no doubt that she was tender from all their lovemaking. As much as he wanted her, he didn't want to hurt her.

She rubbed herself against him again, and Peter moaned.

"You know..." she said, trailing her fingers down his stomach.

Peter sucked in his breath as she curled her fingers around his hardness.

"...even if we have to wait a while for the wedding..." she continued, her voice a sultry whisper as she alternately stroked him and squeezed him. She circled his throbbing tip with her fingernail. "...there's no reason we can't get a head start on the honeymoon...."

When he emerged from the bedroom the next morning, the first rays of sunlight were flickering through the windows like strands of gold, into Aimee's apartment. Opening the French doors, he stepped outside onto the balcony. Even at such an early hour, the thickening humidity made the air feel heavy. Almost as heavy as his conscience over not telling Aimee that he still expected her to sign the prenuptial agreement.

"Morning," Aimee said as she joined him on the balcony. Stretching her arms over her head, she yawned. The silky sage-colored gown outlined the curves of her body as she moved. When she dropped her arms, the fabric flowed over the swell of breasts, the dip at her waist, then fell just above the tips of her bare feet. Her hair was a scattering of thick, dark waves about her head. Her ghost-blue eyes looked huge and sleepy in her small face, her Cupid's-bow mouth soft and kissable. She looked like both an angel and a siren.

And he would have given anything to be able to take her back to bed and make love to her again. Silently Peter mocked his carnal thoughts. Although he had always enjoyed the physical aspects of lovemaking, he had never allowed it to rule his life. He had prided himself on his ability to control his physical urges and not let them control him.

He had never realized how falling in love with someone could completely obliterate the strong element of control he had always employed over himself.

"Hungry?" she asked as she moved into his arms. She rested her head against his chest and slid her arms about his waist. She snuggled against him like a kitten. "I could fix us some breakfast, if you'd like," she offered sleepily.

As his shaft pushed against the zipper of his slacks, Peter smiled to himself. He had most definitely lost any element of control over his body's reaction to Aimee.

Face it, Gallagher, he told himself. With Aimee as his wife he was probably destined to spend the rest of his life in a perennial state of arousal. Not a bad thing at all, he decided. But one that he could do nothing about this morning. "I'll get something at the airport."

"What time's your flight?"

Peter looked at his watch. "It leaves in about three hours. And I still have to go home to pack."

"I'm going to miss you," she said, hugging him tightly.

A strange warmth flooded through him. He couldn't recall ever feeling quite this way before. It was a unique and not at all unpleasant experience to know that she would be thinking of him, anxious for him to return. Somehow it made leaving easier. "I'm going to miss you, too." He brushed his lips against the top of her head. "More than you can imagine. As soon as I get back, we'll wrap up the details on the wedding. Okay?" He hesitated. "And we need to talk about the prenuptial agreement."

She went still in his arms. "I wondered when you were going to mention it. Peter, I—"

"Not now, Aimee. When I get back. We'll talk about it. We'll work it out. I promise." He held his breath and waited for her response.

"All right," she told him. "We'll talk about it when you get back."

Breathing easier, he rushed on. "There'll be all kinds of time changes, but I'll call you every chance I get."

"I'd like that," she said, smiling at him.

His heart beating easier, Peter lowered his mouth to hers. He kissed her, long, deep, memorizing the taste and the texture of her, to carry him through the long days and nights ahead without her.

When he finally lifted his head and looked into her luminous eyes, he whispered, "Forget calling every chance I can. I'm calling you every day."

Twelve

'Have you told Peter, yet?'' Jacques asked Aimee as he worked on a sketch of a woman's face for his next sculpture.

"No," Aimee replied, mixing the paints, in search of the precise shade of pink she wanted. She had been struck with a burst of inspiration since the discovery that she was pregnant last week. The multitude of bright new paintings scattered about her studio were a testament to her creativity and her excitement over the new life growing inside her.

"Why not?"

"Because informing a man he's going to be a father is not the sort of thing you do by telephone.'' Besides, in spite of the fact that Peter had promised to call her every day, she had not heard from him for the past four. "Doris said he's scheduled to return day after tomorrow. I'll tell him face-to-face when he gets home."

"Do you think he will want the child?"

Aimee put down her brush. "Of course he'll want the child. Peter loves children."

"A man can like children and still not want one of his own," Jacques informed her.

At the strange note in his voice, Aimee looked over at Jacques. His eyes were shadowed, and for once there was no trace of the joie de vivre that she always associated with the Frenchman. But before she could question him, he seemed to shake off the odd mood.

"Pay me no mind, *mon amie.* I can see that you are thrilled at the prospect of becoming a mother. I am sure your Peter will be happy, too."

"Yes," Aimee said, trying to squelch the sense of uneasiness that Jacques's comments had evoked. Even though she and Peter had not discussed children, surely he would be just as happy as she was upon learning they were to be parents. She smoothed her fingers over her still-flat stomach, acknowledging for the first time that this was something she and Peter should have discussed.

Jacques came to her side and put his arm around her shoulders. "Come now, little one. Don't let this cynical Frenchman chase away your happiness. Where is that sunshine smile of yours?"

Aimee attempted a smile, but failed miserably as she began to wonder whether Peter's not calling was a sign. Just as his mention of the prenuptial agreement had been a signal that he still did not trust her or her love for him.

"You call that a smile?" Jacques chided. He drew her to the center of the room and, catching her at the waist, he lifted her and spun around in a circle with her in his arms. "You are going to be a mother, Aimee, and I...I will be an uncle. We must celebrate," he said enthusiastically, spinning around with her again.

Aimee tipped her head back and laughed, some of her earlier joy returning.

At the sound of Aimee's laughter, Peter hoisted his travel bag on one shoulder and his briefcase in his other hand and hurried up the last steps to her apartment. He had driven himself to the point of exhaustion over the last few days. But it was worth it, he admitted. Not only had he acquired the

Rubens he had been after, but more importantly, he had been able to cut the trip short and return to Aimee two days sooner than expected.

For once, the sight of her apartment door left ajar didn't bother him. It would make surprising her that much easier. Her laughter floated out to him. Smiling, Peter set down his bags and headed toward the sound of her laughter.

The smile died on his lips the moment he reached her studio. Peter's blood ran cold at the sight that greeted him—his Aimee, in Jacques's arms. An invisible fist seemed to squeeze around his heart and twist in his chest. A paralyzing rage swept through him at her betrayal. He had been a fool. A complete and utter fool.

"Jacques, you idiot, put me down."

"I'd suggest you do as she says," Peter said, his voice as icy and hard as steel.

"Peter!" Aimee disengaged herself from Jacques and raced over to him. She threw her arms around him. "I can't believe you're home. I wasn't expecting you for another two days."

"Obviously."

Oh, she was good, Peter thought as she lifted her smiling face for his kiss. He could almost believe she was happy to see him. Almost. Except for the fact that he had just found her in another man's arms. He had been a fool to believe her, to trust her.

When she brushed her mouth against his, Peter forced himself to remained unmoved. It took every ounce of control he possessed not to crush her to him and return the kiss.

Uneasiness skittered down her spine at Peter's lack of response. Aimee eased back a step and looked at him. He didn't say a word. There was no need to. Peter thought she had betrayed him. The accusation was written in the steely depths of his eyes, in the grim set of his jaw, in the rigid stance of his body.

All the happiness she had experienced when she first saw him standing in the doorway evaporated like a drop of water striking dry sand. And along with her happiness went her foolish dream that Peter did indeed love her. She had deluded herself, Aimee realized. Peter didn't love her. He couldn't. If he did, he would have trusted her. He certainly would not have believed she would betray him.

"Don't be a fool, Gallagher," Jacques began, evidently realizing what Peter thought. "You're jumping to the wrong conclusion."

Fury emanated from Peter, blazed in his eyes.

"Aimee and I were just—"

"Jacques, would you excuse us, please?" Aimee said, silencing her friend.

Jacques hesitated. He looked from Aimee to Peter, then back to Aimee again. "He is like an angry lion, *mon amie*. Let me explain it is not what he thinks."

"No," Aimee told him. She folded her arms across her chest. "No explanations are needed."

"You are sure?"

"Yes," she assured him.

"All right. I will go, then. But be careful. It is not good for you to become upset in your condition."

Peter's gaze shot from Aimee to the door that had just closed behind Jacques. The fist that had been squeezing his heart since he had walked into the studio tightened. He swung his gaze back to Aimee.

Her face, usually so expressive, was as blank as a new canvas when she walked past him. She picked up a paintbrush and began making swift, deliberate strokes across the canvas.

His control shot, Peter stormed over to her and grabbed her wrist, midstroke, splattering drops of pink paint across the painting. "What in the hell did he mean, in your condition?" he demanded.

Aimee looked at the fingers imprisoning her wrist, the same fingers that had loved her, pleasured her. She pushed away the memory. "Let go of me," she commanded, forcing her voice to remain as hard and unfeeling as his. When he released her, Aimee immediately began dabbing at the paint splatters.

"Answer me, Aimee. What did he mean by your condition?"

She looked up at him. "He was referring to the fact that I'm pregnant."

The tight line of his mouth grew even tighter. "Who's the father?"

Aimee flinched. Pain sliced through her with the sharpness of a razor's edge. She shuddered at the utter coldness in his tone. Of all the reactions she could have expected, this had not been one of them.

"Don't look so shocked. Do you think you're the first woman to get herself pregnant with another man's bastard and try to pin it on me? And to think I'd decided to forget about the prenuptial agreement. I thought I could trust you."

"Looks like we were both mistaken," Aimee told him.

Her response seemed to anger him. He pinned her with his steely gaze. "Is the child mine?"

Aimee could feel the color drain from her face. She squeezed her eyes shut at the gut-wrenching pain. She turned away from him, afraid she was going to be sick. What a fool she had been, Aimee told herself. The dream of her, Peter and their child being a family, of the three of them living and loving one another, was just that—a foolish dream. Tears slid silently down her cheeks. She turned around to face him. "Don't worry, Peter. The baby's not yours. It's mine."

His pained expression should have given her some measure of satisfaction. It didn't. Her own anguish was too great.

"Then Gaston's the father."

It was the bitterness in his voice that pushed her over the edge. And in the wake of her anguish came fury. At Peter, for his accusations and his stupidity. At herself, for still loving him. But she no longer had just herself and Peter to think about. Now she had their child to consider. Tipping her chin up, she said, "It's my child." Marching out of the studio, she pulled open the door to her apartment. "Now, I'd like you to go."

Fighting through the haze of anger, Peter followed her, but he ignored the door she held open for him. He studied her pale face, trying to make sense of what she had said. Discovering her with Jacques had infuriated him. The added shock of learning she was pregnant had added to his confusion.

"Please go," she told him again.

Peter looked at her back, stiff and straight. He walked over to the mantel and looked up. The portrait she had painted of him, the one in which she had seen the man he wanted to be. It hung above the mantel, mocking him with the kind, understanding eyes she had given him. He hadn't seen it when he came in earlier. He had been too intent on seeing Aimee, and then too angry upon finding her in Jacques's arms.

She truly did love him, Peter realized as he stared at the finished portrait. It was there for everyone to see, only he had discovered it too late. And much too late he realized it was Aimee's love that he wanted above all things.

Her child, she had said. As the meaning of her words sank in, Peter's heart stuttered. Hope surged through him. This was Aimee. His Aimee. Kind and generous to a fault. And honest. If she had wanted to betray him, to use him, she would have married him first and told him of the child later. She hadn't, because she hadn't betrayed him. She loved him. And he loved her. He went to her. "It's my child, isn't it?"

When she didn't respond, he turned her to face him. "I'm the father, aren't I?" When she still failed to respond, Peter gave her a tiny shake. "Answer me."

"Yes," she finally whispered. "At least technically speaking."

"Technically speaking?"

"Technically you are the father of my child. But it's my child, Peter. Not yours."

"The hell it's not," he said savagely. He crushed her to him. "You're both mine. You and the baby."

Aimee struggled until he released her. "I am not yours, and neither is this baby."

"Of course you are. I'm sorry for jumping to conclusions. I know—"

"It's too late for apologies, Peter. It's over." She pulled off the engagement ring he had had sent to her after leaving that last morning. This time, instead of throwing it at him, she stuffed it in his shirt pocket. "Now, I'd appreciate it if you'd go. Oh, and be sure to close the door on your way out."

"But—"

"Please, Peter. Just go. I really would like to be alone."

He hesitated, but the flatness of her ghost-blue eyes told him there was no point in arguing with her further. At least for the time being. "All right. I'll go—for now."

He would get her back, Peter vowed as he picked up his bags. Somehow, some way, he would make Aimee love him again. And when she belonged to him again, he would never let her go.

"How is my nephew feeling today?" Jacques asked as he swiped an apple from the bowl of fruit on the table in Aimee's studio. He rubbed it on the leg of his pants, then bit into the deep red skin.

"Your niece is feeling fine."

"And what about the little mother?"

"Great," Aimee said, and went back to the painting she had been working on.

"I ran into Peter today."

Aimee's heart skittered at the mention of his name. It had been nearly three weeks since that dreadful day in her studio. Though it had been difficult, she had refused all his calls and attempts to see her. The letters he had sent had been returned unopened. She still loved him desperately, but now she had more than just herself to think about. She had her child to consider. Facing the future as a single parent would be difficult, she told herself. But marrying a man who

didn't love and trust her would have been even more difficult.

"He was a sorry sight. A shadow of the man he once
was," Jacques said before taking another bite of apple. After swallowing, he continued, "Don't you think you're being a little too hard on him? At least talk to him, listen to
what he has to say."

"When did you become such a fan of Peter Gallagher's?"

Jacques shrugged. "Blame it on my French blood. I just
think when two people love each other and are miserable
without one another, they might as well be miserable together."

"Peter doesn't love me."

"How do you know?"

"Because if he loved me, he would have trusted me." The
painful memory of the horrible scene in her studio came
back to her in a rush.

"Did it ever occur to you that it is because he loves you
that he went a little crazy? Doris said he crammed a week's
worth of meetings into three days so he could get back here
to you."

Aimee frowned. "Have you also taken to chatting with
Peter's secretary?"

"I met her at Gallagher's last week, for the special showing of the Rubens. She would have told you as much, if you
would have come with me and Liza, instead of hiding yourself away in here."

"I wasn't hiding."

Jacques finished off the apple and pitched the core in the
trash. He walked over to Aimee and placed his hand upon
her shoulder. His eyes, usually filled with laughter, were
somber. "You can't keep hiding in here forever, Aimee.
Sooner or later, you're going to have to face him. If not for
your own sake, then for the sake of the baby."

"The baby and I don't need him," Aimee replied. She
had gone over it in her head and her heart a hundred times
since that horrible afternoon. While facing the prospect of
being a single parent was somewhat frightening, it would be

easier than facing marriage to a man who didn't love and trust her. Financially, she and the baby would do okay. Business had picked up in the shop and even the building was cooperating.

"Maybe you don't need him, but I suspect Peter needs you." He paused. "You might also want to consider the legal ramifications. After all, the child is Peter's, too."

Aimee's heart froze. "You think he'll sue me for custody?"

"Who knows what lengths a man will go to when he is fighting for what he believes he cannot live without?"

Confused, Aimee didn't know what to say, and before she could even think of a response, Jacques was prowling about her studio. He tilted his head to one side and studied a small abstract of splintered hearts that she had done that morning. The piece was an intense study of vibrant red, bright yellow and deep blue. "Nice. Although it's obvious to me what you were thinking of when you painted this. I think I'll take it to Kay."

"Kay already has a ton of my stuff."

"Not anymore. She sold the last of your paintings this morning."

"That's impossible. I gave her five new pieces just two days ago."

"Gone. Someone came in and took everything she had. I'm on my way over to her place now. I'll bring this one with me."

Aimee was still reeling from the news that all of her paintings had been sold, and it took her a moment to recover. When she did, Jacques was holding *Shattered Hearts* and zeroing in on a half-finished canvas.

"When do you think this one will be finished?" he asked, eyeing the piece, which she had titled *Dreams*.

"I don't have any idea. And you can put down the one you're carrying—the paint is barely dry. Tell Kay I don't have anything to give her."

"You tell her. You're the one who suggested she act as your agent."

"I know," Aimee told him. Following the success of the show and her weekend with Peter, she had opted not to sign on with any gallery, and had approached Kay about representing her work instead. To her surprise, the other woman had accepted. Initially, the sales had been slower, and while the money had been good, the sums had been modest.

Until about a week ago. Then, suddenly, *everything* had begun to sell and at much higher prices. Aimee frowned, growing suspicious. It had also been approximately a week since she had last refused to see or speak to Peter. He hadn't called or contacted her again.

"How long do you think it will take you to finish that one?" Jacques asked, indicating the painting on which she was working.

"Forget it," Aimee told him. "I want you to tell me who this collector is that's suddenly buying all my paintings."

"Haven't got a clue," Jacques said innocently.

"Well, I do," Aimee said, throwing down her brush. All she had ever wanted from Peter was his love and trust—the only things he had refused to give her. "The last time he pulled this stunt, he said he only did it to help me. Well, I didn't want or need his help then, and I don't want or need it now. And I intend to tell him so."

Storming out of her apartment, Aimee headed for Gallagher's. She marched into the gallery, not caring how out of place she looked in her threadbare jeans and paint-stained work shirt.

"Aimee," Doris exclaimed. "It's so good to see you again. I—"

"Where is he?"

"Peter?"

"Yes," Aimee replied, growing more irritated by the minute. What had Peter hoped to accomplish by buying her paintings? Did he really believe he could buy his way back into her life, and that of their child? Didn't he know that his money meant nothing to her?

"He's in the vault."

"Thanks. I know the way." Aimee sped down the corridor to the private chamber where Peter housed his most precious works. She couldn't help remembering the last time she had entered the room, when she had spied the painting of the ballet slippers. She swallowed, recalling the story Peter had told her about his parents. That day, for the first time, she had understood the demons that drove him. She shoved the memory aside, refusing to allow herself to soften.

The door to the vault opened just as she reached it. "Come in, Aimee," Peter said, as though he were expecting her.

"You knew I would come, didn't you?" It galled her that she had responded to his bait.

"I hoped you would." He pulled the door shut and punched some numbers. Something bleeped, and a red light flickered on.

"What are you doing?" She struggled a moment to see as her eyes adjusted to the dim lighting.

"Activating the alarm. My most valuable possessions are in here. I don't want to risk losing them." He flipped a switch and lights flooded the wall, illuminating the painting of his mother's ballet slippers.

Jacques was right, Aimee thought. Peter didn't look the same. He had lost weight, and even in the unnatural light of the vault she could see the shadows under his eyes.

He flipped another switch, revealing the two Rubenses. His fingers worked another row of switches and the entire wall lit up, a burst of bright light illuminating her paintings.

Aimee spun around. Her paintings covered the walls, rested side by side with the Rubens, a Matisse, a Monet. Masterpieces, priceless works of art. His most valuable possessions, Peter had said, and he had placed her paintings among them.

"Why, Peter? Why did you buy my paintings? And don't tell me you did it to help me, I'm doing fine on my own."

"I know you are. And I didn't buy them to help you. I bought them as an investment."

"We both know that's not true."

"But it is true. I intend to have quite an extensive collection of works by the brilliant new artist from New Orleans, Aimee Lawrence. In fact, I intend to hold an exhibit showcasing my collection of her works."

"It's not going to work, Peter."

"No? I think you're wrong, Aimee. Because I intend to make a small fortune on these paintings."

She scoffed.

"It's true. Trust me. I have an eye for what sells, and I will make a fortune with your work. My only regret is that I didn't start buying your paintings before now. My only excuse is that I was too blinded by my feelings to use good business sense. But then, I guess it's not every day that I fall in love with an artist." He paused. "And I *do* love you, Aimee."

Though she tried not to respond, Aimee could feel the hope beginning to stir inside her again. She looked away from his mesmerizing eyes and at the wall of paintings. "Why are my paintings in here?"

"Because they're invaluable to me. Just like the woman who painted them."

Aimee couldn't help but feel pleasure at his words. "What about my baby?"

"Our baby," Peter said. "I want you both."

"Wanting's not enough, Peter."

"What about loving you? Because I do love you, Aimee."

Aimee shook her head. "You can't love without trust, Peter. If you loved me, you would never have doubted me."

"It wasn't you I doubted. It was myself. I didn't believe I was deserving of your love. And when I came to your apartment that day so anxious to see you, I thought I would die right then and there when I saw you in Jacques's arms. I was so eaten up with jealousy, so sick at losing you to him, that I lashed out at you. By the time I got my temper under control, it was too late. I'd said some horrible things, cruel things. Things I couldn't take back. And then you refused to speak to me."

"So you started buying all of my paintings, just so I would speak to you?"

"That was part of it."

She waited for him to continue.

"I told you—it made good business sense. Trust me, Aimee. Despite my stupidity where your work is concerned, I do know what sells. Launching you makes good sense from a business standpoint. And I do intend to launch you. Someday the rest of the world is going to recognize your talent."

Still unconvinced, Aimee asked, "What happens if I become a star? Aren't you afraid that I'll run off, the way Leslie did?"

"I'll admit, the thought had crossed my mind. But I'm hoping you won't." He smiled at her then, with all the warmth and hope in his heart. "If you still love me half as much as I love you, it shouldn't be a problem. Because you and our baby are all that matter to me. Do you still love me, Aimee? Or have I managed to kill everything you felt for me?"

His doubt and uncertainty touched her deep in her soul. "I love you, Peter," she whispered. "I've never stopped."

Peter crushed her to him then, and kissed her with all the love in his heart. "Will you marry me?"

"Yes," she whispered, kissing him back.

"I don't want to wait. I know a judge who will give us a special license. We can get married again in a church and have a reception for your family and friends later, if you'd like. But I don't want to wait any longer."

Aimee hesitated. "What about the prenuptial agreement?"

"We don't need one."

"What happens if things don't work out? Suppose we got divorced? Aren't you afraid of losing the gallery? I know how much Gallagher's means to you."

"Not half as much as you do. The gallery, and a dozen Rubenses and Monets, would be worthless to me without you and our child. You and our baby are all that matter to me. Besides," he said, holding her close, "I have every intention of this marriage being a very long and happy one."

"Me too," she told him.

Peter flipped off the light switches illuminating the art, sending the room into darkness, save for the lamp on his desk. And as the darkness enveloped them, this time Peter had no fear—not with Aimee, his light, by his side.

*   *   *   *   *

SILHOUETTE® *Desire®*

COMING NEXT MONTH

#979 MEGAN'S MARRIAGE—Annette Broadrick
Daughters of Texas
February's *Man of the Month* and Aqua Verde County's most
eligible bachelor, Travis Hanes, wanted Megan O'Brien as his
bride. And now that she needed his help, could Travis finally talk
stubborn Megan into being the wife he wanted?

#980 ASSIGNMENT: MARRIAGE—Jackie Merritt
Tuck Hannigan had to pose as pretty Nicole Currie's husband if
he was going to protect her. Could this phony marriage get the
confirmed bachelor thinking about a honeymoon for real?

#981 REESE: THE UNTAMED—Susan Connell
Sons and Lovers
Notorious playboy Reese Marchand knew mysteriously sexy
Beth Langdon was trouble. But he couldn't stay away from the
long-legged beauty—even if it meant revealing his long-kept
secret.

#982 THIS IS MY CHILD—Lucy Gordon
Single dad Giles Haverill was the only man who could help
Melanie Haynes find the baby she'd been forced to give up
years ago. Unfortunately, he was also the one man she could
never love....

#983 DADDY'S CHOICE—Doreen Owens Malek
Taylor Kirkland's goal in life was to regain custody of his
daughter. But then he met Carol Lansing—an irresistible woman
whose love could cost him that dream....

#984 HUSBAND MATERIAL—Rita Rainville
Matthew Flint never thought he would make a good husband—
until he lost the only woman he ever loved. Now he would do
anything to convince Libby Cassidy he really was husband
material.

FRIENDS, LOVERS...AND BABIES
by Joan Elliott Pickart

Joan Elliott Pickart brings her own special brand of
humor to these heartwarming tales of the MacAllister
men. For these three carefree bachelors, predicting the
particulars of the MacAllister babies is much easier
than predicting when wedding bells will sound!

In February 1996, the most romantic month of
the year. Ryan MacAllister discovers true love—and
fatherhood—in *Friends, Lovers...and Babies*,
book two of THE BABY BET.

And in April 1996, Silhouette Special Edition
brings you the final story of love and surprise
from the MacAllister clan.

BABBET2

Coming in 1996 from

SILHOUETTE®

Desire®

SONS AND *Lovers*

A new series by three of romance's hottest authors

January—LUCAS: THE LONER by Cindy Gerard

February—REESE: THE UNTAMED by Susan Connell

March—RIDGE: THE AVENGER by Leanne Banks

SONS AND *Lovers* : Three brothers denied a father's name, but granted the gift of love from three special women.

"For the best mini-series of the decade, tune into SONS AND LOVERS, a magnificent trilogy created by three of romance's most gifted talents."
—Harriet Klausner
Affaire de Coeur

SLOVERS

**Trained to protect, ready to lay their
lives on the line, but unprepared for
the power of love.**

Award-winning author Beverly Barton brings you
Ashe McLaughlin, Sam Dundee and J. T. Blackwood...
three rugged, sexy ex-government agents—each with a
special woman to protect.

Embittered former DEA Agent Sam Dundee has a chance at
romance in GUARDING JEANNIE, IM #688, coming in January
1996. Hired to protect Jeannie Alverson, the woman who saved
his life years ago, Sam is faced with his greatest challenge
ever...guarding his heart and soul from her loving, healing
hands.

And coming in April 1996, the trilogy's exciting conclusion.
Look for J. T. Blackwood's story, BLACKWOOD'S WOMAN,
IM #707.

To order your copy of the first book in THE PROTECTORS series, Ashe McLaughlin's
story, DEFENDING HIS OWN (IM #670), please send your name, address, zip or
postal code along with a check or money order (please do not send cash) for $3.75
($4.25 in Canada) plus 75¢ postage and handling ($1.00 in Canada), payable to
Silhouette Books, to:

In the U.S.	In Canada
Silhouette Books	Silhouette Books
3010 Walden Ave.	P. O. Box 636
P. O. Box 9077	Fort Erie, Ontario
Buffalo, NY 14269-9077	L2A 5X3

Please specify book title(s) with your order.
Canadian residents add applicable federal and provincial taxes.   BBPROT2

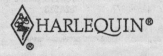